John B Spencer

was born in west London, where he still lives with his wife Lou, and the youngest of their three sons. He is a much-respected musician, record producer and songwriter and has released a number of CDs. This is his sixth novel.

Tooth
&
Nail

John B Spencer

BLOODLINES

First Published in Great Britain in 1998 by
The Do-Not Press
PO Box 4215
London SE23 2QD

A Paperback Original

Copyright © 1998 by John B Spencer
The right of John B Spencer to be identified as the Author of this work has been asserted by him in accordance with the Copyright, Designs & Patents Act 1988.

ISBN 1 899344 31 4

British Library Cataloguing in Publication Data. A catalogue record for this book is available from the British Library.

All rights reserved. No part of this publication may be reproduced, transmitted or stored in a retrieval system, in any form or by any means without the express permission in writing of The Do-Not Press having first been obtained.

This book is sold on the condition that it shall not, by way of trade or otherwise, be lent, resold or hired out or otherwise circulated without the publisher's prior consent in any form of binding or cover other than that in which it is published and without a similar condition being imposed on the subsequent purchaser.

Printed and bound in Great Britain by The Guernsey Press Co Ltd.

h g f e d c b a

To J-J-Jim.

This is a work of fiction and all the characters represented are responsible for their own attitudes and opinions. Any offence… take it up with those characters.

They are out there, somewhere.

ACKNOWLEDGMENTS
Syd, Tom, Lou, Jim D, William, Jimmy B, Ginge, Shirley, Janene, Stormin' Norman on Eleven South.

Thank you.

PART ONE
Sounds Reasonable...

Mrs Kalpana Chatterji would have died in her sleep, smoke inhalation, had it not been for the cystitis irritating her bladder, waking her with the need to pee at two o' clock, her husband, Amit, asleep on his back, taking up much of the bed, arms outstretched, snoring. Kalpana, dressing-gown over her nightdress, feeling the heat as she opened the bedroom door, a dry heat, a scorching heat, reminding her of when she was a small child in Salimpur, before the rains came in February... hearing a noise she could not identify, like the rushing of the wind, then, at the top of the stairs, staring, unable to believe the sea of flame, the hallway below a fiery vortex, hungry for oxygen, swirling, dragging her down towards the conflagration. Screaming without sound, softer than the mew of a cat, as she voided her bladder, the warm urine running down her legs, over her bare feet, soaking into the carpet, Kalpana running back along the narrow upstairs hallway to the children's bedroom... Najeeta and Haresh. Remembering the film Amit had watched on the television, Kalpana saying to him, 'I do not think it is good that Najeeta see this, she will have nightmares,' tower block burning, the actor throwing a chair, breaking a window, sucked out through the shattered glass into the darkness of the night, many floors above the ground... outside the children's bedroom door, now, holding it shut, crying, the paint on the door blistering, shouting, 'Do not open this door... do not open this door,' over and over... the bedroom window just a short drop to the flat roof of the kitchen below, praying to Brahma – Allah, Jesus Christ, even, if any God would save her children – that Najeeta, seven years-old yesterday, they had bought her that new Japanese toy, you must press buttons to feed it, otherwise it will die... will take little Haresh in her arms, jump from the window.

Smoke and heat filling her lungs.

Aware that she is now on her knees.

Najeeta standing in the bedroom door, her nightdress and her mother's raven hair bursting into flames as the vortex swept over them seeking the cool night air beyond the open bedroom window.

Haresh, gripping the edge of his cot, illuminated in the flames...

Then lost to the black smoke.

1

Darren Friend was in no mood to be listening to this snotty bitch... her at the other end of the line, kumquat firmly lodged in her mouth, saying, 'Of course, we've had a number of quotes to consider but we've decided to go with yours.'

Darren thinking, Do me no favours.

Patronising...

Or what?

This, after just coming off the phone to that cow from the Hammersmith VAT Office, giving him a hard time, always on his back every second of every fucking day. Ms Joy Shanks – Darren didn't believe a word of it – saying, 'You do appreciate, Mr Friend, that we have a statutory right to insist, if necessary?' Alison, from the other desk, big grin on her face, listening while Darren pleaded a further ten days' grace, saying, after he had slammed the phone down, 'Do I gather my days of gainful employment with this organisation might be numbered?'

Darren saying, 'And you find that so amusing?'

Alison, she liked to tease him, fuck knows why he let her get away with it all the time, saying, 'I did warn you, Darren; that seventeen and a half per cent is just not your money.'

'What am I, some glorified tax collector?'

'I'll come visit, bring you in your favourite falafel on pitta from across the road, loads of chilli.'

Now this fucking bitch.

Three bay window panels.

Toughened glass in sealed units.

Focal point of the whole fucking universe.

Darren thinking, Stick it right in your ear, darling, but saying, 'Well, that's very nice, I'm sure it's a decision you won't regret.'

Doodling on his pad.

The woman saying, 'When do you think you can make a start?'

Two enormous boobs, erect nipples, lines radiating out from them, like you would get from lighted bulbs in a cartoon. Drawing a circle for the head, adding a smile, two dots for the nostrils, two more dots for the eyes, with long lashes, big hair, thought-bubble, reading, 'And how may I help you, sir?'

Alison, watching him, saying, 'You're losing it, Darren.'

The woman – Darren knowing what was coming next – saying, 'We do need the work completed rather urgently. My builder has promised to be out of the house by Thursday week.'

My builder.

Fucking tart.

Darren now leafing through the order book, going back six weeks before he found the estimate. Six weeks to make up her mind, now she wants it yesterday, saying to the woman, 'Thirty-two Belvedere?'

Mrs Reece-Morgan, placing her now, mobile glued to her ear, checking details with her old man, the house gutted from top to bottom, serious money involved... remembering he had added fifty notes for the double-barrel, another fifty for the address, row of terraced houses, bricks and mortar not much to write home about, but close to the river, her husband something in property... Her saying, that day he went round to view the job, 'Oh God, no, we don't intend to be living here ourselves.'

Darren, mentally, adding another fifty.

Aware that he would be getting a look from Alison, saying now, over the phone, 'Of course, there's the VAT to add to that.'

The woman saying, 'Perhaps, we could come to some arrangement for cash?'

'Not possible, I'm afraid. My accountant would shop me, himself.'

Always looking for a deal.

The more they had the less they enjoyed parting with it.
'Could we make it a round sum?'
Nine hundred and seventy-two.
Plus fitting.
Plus VAT.
Darren saying, 'How about a round thousand?'
The woman saying, 'Inclusive?'
Missing Darren's joke.
Darren saying, 'No offence, Mrs Reece-Morgan, but we're not family, we're not friends. If I was to approach you in the street, a perfect stranger, ask you to give me three hundred pounds, how would you react?'
'I should probably tell you to sod off.'
'Exactly, Mrs Reece-Morgan. It's an honest quote, it's a realistic quote… I'm afraid you're going to have to take it or leave it.'
Alison rolling her eyes.
Heard it all before.
Darren going back to the doodle, adding an hourglass figure, belly-button, bush of pubic hair.
Legs…
He was hopeless at legs.
The woman sighing, saying, 'Then, perhaps you would be so good as to give me an honest and realistic time-frame for the job?'
Sarcastic bitch.
'My fitter will be out of there before your builder, I can promise you that.'
'You'll let me know when he's coming?'
'Personally.'
Then: 'We'll need a third deposit before we can start… say, four hundred?'
The woman capitulating.
Long sigh.
Game, set and match.
'It will be in the post.'
'I'll look forward to that.'
Alison applauding as he cradled the phone.
Saying, 'Masterful.'

Darren thinking, Four hundred, twelve hundred, a piss in the ocean... Get Stoney in on the glazing, Stoney wouldn't hassle him for the money, not Stoney, weak little shit.

The glass suppliers, they could go fuck themselves.

Better still, they could go fuck Ms Joy Shanks and her statutory right to insist.

Alison...

He felt bad about Alison.

Saying to her, now, How would you like to sit on my face?'

2

Lindsay drew comfort from the fact that at least she and Duncan had drifted together on the same raft of ennui, each of them, at every turn, settling for the easy option, no *grand passion*, no flames of desire, requited or otherwise, to conflagrate the cosy fabric of their lives together.

Of course, there had been other men, three to be exact – at the age of forty-seven it would hardly have demonstrated her passivity for it to have been otherwise – each of these flings, 'fling' itself too strong a word, just another manifestation of going with the flow, embracing the easy option…

David and Martin, six years apart, both of them on Support Agency seminar's at the Shalimar Lodge in Buckinghamshire, both of them, after Saturday night drinks in the hotel bar, room keys on the table, easier to accept than refuse. Both of them, like herself, married.

Martin, later, making it difficult in the work-place.

Opening windows.

Poorly concealed messages.

Lindsay, taking advantage of a ministerial level downsizing directive, having him transferred out of the department.

And that three week trip to Paros with her mother, just before she lost her mobility, went into hospital for the last time, died without privacy in a mixed ward on the eleventh floor at Charing Cross Hospital, renal failure… Lindsay bored senseless on that last obligatory trip to the sun.

A Greek waiter.

Was she really that mind-numbingly predictable.

Spiros.

Oh God!

If only his name had been anything but Spiros.

Duncan saying, when she got back from the trip, 'You look as if you could do with a holiday.'

Lindsay saying, 'Spare me, three weeks on a Greek Island with my bloody mother... thank Christ I'm back at work tomorrow.'

Duncan laughing.

'Don't say I didn't warn you,' he said.

Three weeks apart. A brief hug, kisses exchanged.

On the cheek.

Spiros, his breath stinking of Metaxas Brandy, between her legs, 'Sa-gha-po... you say that?' Lindsay repeating each syllable to the rhythm of his body, 'Sa-gha-po... Sa-gha-po,' wondering whether it was too soon for her to cry out, fake her orgasm, precipitate his climax.

Spiros licking the sweat from her breasts.

The heat in the tiny room unbearable.

Saying, 'I love you, that is what it means... sa' ghapo.'

Lindsay saying, 'I'd better get back to my room, my mother may be awake.'

His dark stubble abrasive against the swell of her stomach, pink from the sun... what had she been thinking of, with her figure, wearing a bikini? Wondering if she might have dared to go topless, her mother not there, sun-lounge chair and parasol hired daily, her favourite spot on the beach, reading the Barbara Cartland she had bought at Heathrow.

Theft of a Heart.

Not sure if she had read it before.

The beach just across the road from the Hotel Laskarina where they had a twin room on the first floor, en suite, balcony overlooking the sea. Rebetika drifting up through the papyrus-thatched veranda from the hotel taverna below. Spiro saying, on the third evening, after Lindsay's mother was settled in bed, Lindsay downstairs in the taverna bar, ordering her second ouzo, 'It is the true music of Greece... Rebetika.' Then telling her about the cats, scrounging food at the tables, so many of them, all young. Spiros laughing, saying, 'End of season, black sacks, into the ocean.' Lindsay horrified, Spiros saying, 'Without the tourists they would starve... it is a kindness.'

Spittle and brandy, a marinade co-mingling with the spill of his ejaculation. His tongue, the tongue of a doomed island cat, lapping at a bowl of milk. Lindsay hoping that he wasn't going to kiss her on the mouth when he was through.

Watching an enormous bug.

Crawling across the ceiling.

And Duncan, now, quiet all through dinner – salmon steaks from the supermarket with *tagliatella* and bobby beans; been like this for weeks, saying, 'There's something I ought to tell you.'

Lindsay saying, 'I don't think that's really necessary, do you, Duncan?'

'You haven't heard what I'm going to say, yet.'

'Do I need to?'

Duncan, nine-to-five mentality. Advertising manager on the local newspaper, the *West London Post*, developing a work ethic, staying late... the name, Carol, coming up in his conversation, edited the music column, Leicester University, degree in English Literature, kids had to take anything they could get these days, Duncan saying things like, 'There's been a total revolution, these girls...'

'Girls?'

'Well, okay, women.'

'And what about these women?'

Duncan: 'They're just so upfront, so positive.'

'Make all the running?'

'Well... yes.'

Lindsay saying, then: 'Duncan, you're such a fool.'

Tired of his preoccupation.

Carol this.

Carol that.

Clearing away the dishes, scrapping the salmon bones into the kitchen bin, coming back to the table with a lemon torte, two bowls, two spoons. Duncan saying, 'I'm a bit full up for pudding. That salmon...'

'Coffee?'

'Lindsay...'

The smell of the fish reminding Lindsay of the Greek Island cats.
Paros.
Spiros.'
'It was good?'
'Better than your husband?'
Men...
Why were they so bloody stupid?
Saying to Spiros, 'It was different, that's all.'
Saying to Duncan...
'Duncan, I don't want to know, okay?'

3

The bizarrest thing, how Stoney Todd ended up breaking up with his old lady, Grace. They'd been at the kitchen table, talking after dinner one Sunday evening, dishes in the sink, kettle on the boil for Grace to do the washing-up, talking about this and that, the conversation moving around the way conversations do, Stoney, half his attention on the telly guide in *The Mirror*, seeing if there wasn't a half-way decent film on the box tonight, something with Bruce Willis or Arnie Schwarzenegger, a film worth staying in for, not get stuck in The Mason's all fucking night with Dennis and Kevin... Grace saying it was probably a good thing they were both always skint, the problems money caused, especially if someone had died not leaving a will, the families at each other's throats over it, Stoney chiming in that she was not only right that they were always skint but, even if they did have money...

There would never be any kids... not unless they adopted.

Stoney's fault, not Grace's.

Low sperm count.

The young Indian doctor at Ealing Hospital, after the test results, talking them through the alternatives, something called IVF, a long procedure, would cost two thousand pounds, or thereabouts, no guarantee of success. Both Stoney and Grace thinking, Two thousand quid?

Fuck that for a game of soldiers.

Grace pointing out that while they might not have any kids of their own, there were cousins on both sides, out of touch for years, but it was surprising what could come crawling out of the woodwork, the possibility of something for nothing...

And we do have the house.

Stoney always forgetting they had the house, owned it lock stock and barrel, took it for granted that him and Grace never had a problem making the rent every week, get kicked out on their arses if they fell too far behind... the house bought outright with money left to Grace by her father, three bedrooms, garden front and back, the old Cortina 2.00 GL X Reg, up on blocks in the front, Stoney promising himself he was going to fix it up some day, the house in Pope's Lane, not so valuable since the road had got busy with traffic, but still, worth a bob or two. Grace's father, Ted, crafty old bastard he was... left Grace's mother, out of the blue, back in 1953, Grace, the only child, just three years old at the time. Grace's mother, Phyllis, knocked down and killed by a bus in the Fulham Palace Road, in '74, on her way to Charing Cross Hospital for a check-up on her rheumatoid arthritis... that's how Stoney remembered her, always hobbling about with a walking stick, her knees all bandaged up. Ted dying of a stroke in '76, living out in Datchet with his new Polish woman, Katya, never married her, which was lucky for Grace and Stoney. Going through the papers, after the funeral out at Ruislip Crematorium, they discovered *just* what a crafty old bastard Ted had been, won twenty-seven thousand six-hundred on the Littlewoods Football Pools three weeks before he left Phyllis, never breathed a word of it to anyone, especially Phyllis. The money in his account enough for Grace and Stoney to buy the house in Pope's Lane, the only sensible thing they'd done in their whole lives, the both of them partial to a few drinks, not wanting to piss it all up the wall...

Have nothing left to show for it.

The Polish woman, Katya, took Grace to court over it but lost. Nobody had ever heard of palimony in 1976, and, anyway, she already owned the house in Datchet. Ted, tight bastard that he was, had left his winnings intact, not touched a penny, building up interest in the bank, Phyllis, meanwhile struggling to bring up Grace on her own, all the judge's sympathy going with Grace, not Katya.

Besides...

She was Polish.

Stoney, at the kitchen table, not knowing why he came out with it, but wishing to God he hadn't, saying to Grace, 'But, if we ever split up, not that I'm saying it's likely, but, *if* we ever did, it would be obvious we'd have to sell the house. It wouldn't be fair, one of us living here rent free, the other one struggling to make ends meet in some shit-house of a bed-sit, because that's all either of us could ever afford… we're, neither of us, up to holding down a regular job, let's face it.'

Grace, just started on the washing-up, coming back to the table dripping soap suds, saying, 'You'd do that to me! Force me to sell the house, paid for with my own father's money?'

Stoney saying, 'Grace, I'm only saying *if*.'

'How could you even think such a thing?'

'Grace…'

'You'd leave me without a fucking roof over my head? No provision for the future, nothing to pass on when I go?'

Building up a head of steam.

Stoney saying, 'When you go? For fuck's sake, Grace, you're only forty-six,' trying to lighten things up, 'Still turning a few heads, in case you hadn't noticed.'

'Just what kind of fucking bastard are you?'

Stoney trying to be reasonable, pointing out that he had only been talking, that he wasn't about to go and leave her… why the fuck should he want to do that?

All of which cut no ice with Grace.

Off on one with a vengeance.

Next thing, he was out of the house.

Explaining what had happened to Dennis and Kevin, Mason's Arms, usual table opposite where they sold hot food at lunch-time, office workers in from all the companies along the Great West Road, next to the overpass.

Asking Kevin if he could kip out on his settee till he got sorted, which wasn't going to go down too well with Kevin's new missus, Monica, what with the baby on the way, could be any time now.

Stoney saying, 'Women… I ask you.'

Dennis saying, 'Look on the bright side, Stoney, leastways now, you can go ahead and do it, get some money in your bin for once.'

Stoney saying, 'Do what?'
'Divorce her, you toss-pot, get her to sell the house.'
Stoney, looking at Dennis, saying, 'Me do that to Grace?
'What kind of a bastard do you take me for?'
'Wonderwall', Oasis, coming up on the jukebox.
Dennis and Kevin exchanging glances.
Dennis saying, 'Your shout, Stoney, I do believe.'

4

Darren had six CDs loaded on the sound system in the boot of the XJ6, every one of them Elvis Presley, Country Hits playing now, 'Green Grass of Home', eat your heart out Tom Jones…

As I wake and look around me,
At the four grey walls that surround me…

Nosing the silver-grey bonnet into the Bush Green, a number 11, woman driving, letting him in, wonders would never fucking cease, Darren tapping the horn to acknowledge, other drivers looking round at the Jag, giving him the look, you got a problem, or what, The King, nothing over the top, every note for real, Darren right there with him in that prison cell, feeling all the pain, all the longing…

Still pissing down.

Blowers keeping the windscreen clear, wipers on full.

Six-thirty, Tuesday evening.

Darren amazed how many people there were missed the whole fucking point of the song… wondering about the execution, how they did it – lethal injection, cyanide pellets, the electric chair, The King strapped to the hot seat, flames bursting from beneath the straps, black smoke filling the chamber, the Pelvis going into convulsions, like he wanted to be up out of that seat one last time, right leg twitching, mind of its own, right hand gripping the mike stand, left hand flung out across the crowd of screaming kids…

Doing the dance.

Hayride, Louisiana.

Circa '56.

Easing into the outside lane, next to the green, junction with Wood Lane and the Uxbridge Road up ahead, traffic hardly moving, Darren looking out over the Green, wondering where all the dossers went when it was coming down like this…

Green, green grass of home.

Shepherd's Bush Green.

Thinking about Mary.

'Minge quite hairy…' that's what they sang, back when they were still at school, knowing the song despite it had been a hit, the Tom Jones version, while Darren was still in nappies.

Mary…

Crying in the chapel.

Down on her knees praying as the prison governor threw the switch, dimmed the lights. Darren wanting to know the rest of the story, whether she ever got over it, married, settled down, had kids. Turning off the CD player as the track finished, thinking, Knowing women, probably spreading her fucking legs inside a fortnight. Picking up the mobile from the passenger seat, Reggie answering on the third ring, Darren saying, 'Wonders will never cease.'

Reggie saying, 'Darren.'

'I've been trying to reach you all afternoon.'

'Well, now you did.'

'I've been giving it some thought… the other night.'

Reggie saying, 'And?'

Darren touching the accelerator, coming up alongside a red Post Office van – mad fuckers, all of them – allowing the van to cut a path out ahead of him into the junction with Wood Lane, the Green still on his right, heading east, now, towards Shepherd's Bush Roundabout, checking the mirror to get into the middle lane, avoid the tail-back of traffic doing a right at the end of the Green. Queues of people at the bus stops on the far side of the road, women with shopping, office workers still on the way home, standing in the rain. Bunch of black kids outside McDonald's, shell-suits, hoods up, gobbing on the pavement. Chinese and Indian takeaways doing good business, everybody, apart from the black kids, in a hurry to get indoors, dry off, get stuck into *Eastenders*. Darren thinking, if the Mitchell brothers were light relief, what the fuck was the world coming to…

Saying to Reggie, 'We need to talk some more.'

'In the motor?'

'Bush Green.'

Reggie saying, 'This bloke rang me once, on his mobile. Mid-sentence went smack into the back of a Tesco Supermarket lorry... air-bag goes off, bloke screaming, that horrible grinding sound you get when two lumps of metal keep on coming at each other. Phone still on send, heard everything. Him groaning, sirens, fire brigade cutting him out with an acetylene torch, him screaming fit to wake the dead when the paramedics shifted him... fascinating, it was.'

'I'm sure it was, Reggie.'

'I rang his missus. She said the doctors did everything they could but, well, there you go.'

Then: 'Eyes front at all times, am I right, Darren?'

'You say so, Reggie.'

'I do say so, Darren. Could have yourself a nasty accident.'

'Chance would be a fine thing.'

Making the middle lane.

Seven hundred and eighty-three a month for the motor, plus fully comp' insurance, three months behind, already, girl on the phone from Norton-Hamblin Financing every other day. 'Did you receive our letter?' – pronounced 'lett-*are*' – '... account in good ord-*are*... if you would ring me back on this numb-*are*.' Alison and Darren falling about laughing, listening to the playback on the answer machine, too good to be true when she said, 'Just ask for Patric-*are*.' Patric-*are* Well-*are*, credit control department, Norton-Hamblin Finance. Lease, don't buy, his accountant had advised him. What was the fucking point of tax deductible...

Deductible from what?

'Or the Old Bill on your back... due care and attention.'

Darren, across Shepherd's Bush Roundabout, into Holland Park Avenue, traffic solid all the way up the hill, wondering if he should call Kiren, tell her he was running late – how late would depend on Reggie – saying to Reggie, 'I was heading in your direction.'

'On the off-chance.'

'I'm meeting Kiren. Chinese in Queensway.'

Mr Poon. Best wind-dried duck in London. Kiren always went for the Singapore Noodles. Liked picking up the fat tiger prawns with her fingers, licking her fingers afterwards.

'Kiren? What happened to Zoë?'

'I met Kiren, that's what happened to Zoë.'

'I rather liked Zoë.'

'Give her a call, I'm sure she'd fall about laughing.'

'You think so?'

'I know so. Zoë likes it straight, and that's something you can't manage unless you're hanging by the neck from the fucking ceiling.'

Darren had looked it up one time, after Reggie had told him, couldn't believe anybody would want to do such a weirdo thing... paraphilia. Choke off the oxygen supply to the brain, orgasm like nothing you could imagine.

According to Reggie.

Darren had said, 'I'm going to have to take your word for it on that one, Reggie,' saying, now, 'I find a space, I can be with you in ten minutes.'

'Why the change of heart, Darren?'

'Needs must...'

'When the Devil drives?'

'Something like that, Reggie. '

Reggie laughing.

'Just glad I'm able to help out.'

Darren saying, 'I'll need some up-front.'

'And you shall have it.'

'Now... this evening?'

'I don't see why not... don't forget, Darren, top bell. I'll be listening out.'

Top bell.

Reggie's place, five storey mid-Victorian terraced house in Stanley Crescent, overlooking the gardens... big rooms, rococo plasterwork, tall ceilings, tall enough for Reggie to hang himself by the neck until dead any time he wanted. Reggie, before he moved in, had had the place converted from five self-contained units, back to its original condition, kept the front door intercom system, five bells, five nameplates, grill to speak into, assure the tenant you weren't a house-breaker, Jehovah

Witness, bailiff come to serve a Notice of Distress and Inventory, Reggie keeping all the same names except the top one, changed that to R. Crystal.

Reggie's idea of a joke.

Wasn't fooling anyone.

Expensive drapes in every window.

Pristine paintwork.

No pile of junk mail inside the front door.

Bicycles chained up by the basement steps.

Reggie breaking the connection. Darren, at the lights by Holland Park Station, indicating, turning left into Landsdowne Road, right into Ladbroke Road, looking for an empty bay, Nissan Bluebird pulling out from a space just ahead.

Luck be my lady.

Darren, parked up, out of the car, turning back to lock the doors, Jaguar giving him a farewell beep, flash of the hazards.

Walking fast.

Still pissing it down.

Back with Elvis Presley, the 'Green Green Grass of Home', head down, humming the tune.

The pain and longing in The King's voice.

The regret.

Wondering if the electric chair was the same as hanging…

Going to your grave…

Come stains round your crutch?

5

Carol talking about the band she had seen last night, saying they were post-modernist. Duncan thinking, What wasn't post-modernist these days? Bench-table overlooking the towpath, Kew Bridge up river, south-bound traffic not moving, visible above the parapet.

Duncan drinking London Pride, straight glass.

Carol, Labatt Ice, no glass.

Carol saying, 'On the surface they sound like any other light-weight pop band, but, there's an underlying irony. It's like they've assimilated the genre and now they're taking the piss... and the lead singer, he's drop-dead gorgeous.'

Duncan watching the swans.

A rowing eight, far bank, skulling, blades dripping water, symmetrical eddies in the wake of the craft, the water high, placid, on the turn.

Duncan not able to look her in the eye, feeling like a kid, saying, 'What did you say they were called?'

Carol saying, 'The Conflabs.'

Duncan, making a joke, saying, 'The Flab Four?'

Carol saying, 'There's five of them... the bass player's a girl.'

As if that made any difference to Duncan.

'Comes from round here, Teddington, that's why I writing them up.'

'Did you do an interview?'

'With the lead singer... totally out of his head, I'd have loved some of what he was on. He said they were all going for an Indian afterwards, them and their manager, asked me if I wanted to come.'

'And, did you?'

'Give me credit, he's only twenty. Besides, he was too full of himself by far.'

Carol, twenty-six.

Six years, at that age, a lifetime.

Duncan, forty-nine, the lift home from Richmond to Chiswick, if Carol was still in the office, not out working on something, now routine, signifying nothing... this, the first time he had asked her if she wanted to stop off, have a drink by the river.

The weather now clear.

Still not warm for the time of the year.

Duncan had taken weeks to ask.

Saying, now, 'I have a problem with post-modern... it seems to me that if modern is up-to-date, then post-modern must mean the future... pure semantics, I know.'

Carol saying, 'It's retro, but...' thinking about it, then saying, 'It's like... taking something from the past, but investing it indelibly with the here and now, the retro aspect becomes a virtual reality... like the Bootleg Beatles are retro, Oasis are post-modern.'

'You mean the way the breweries rip the guts out of a perfectly respectable pub, turn it into an *Oirish* theme pub, lousy acoustics, chairs you can't sit on, shamrock in the top of your Guinness, ask the New Zealander behind the bar for a glass – not a pint – and he won't know what the fuck you are talking but?'

Aware that Carol didn't know the difference between a glass and a pint, either, despite she had a friend from university, living in Waterford with her boyfriend, Carol visited them, regularly. Duncan remembering what his friend had said, Allan, used to play chess once a week, go for a drink afterwards... left his wife and three children for a woman half his age, went skulking back after only three months. 'It's all the footnotes, having to explain everything gets you down after a while.'

Duncan adding, 'Today's special, lasagne and wholewheat bap roll.'

Carol laughing.

Off the hook on the 'glass.'

Saying, 'You won't believe this, but it's the God's honest truth... I was in this bar in Dungarvan, everybody said it was the place to go for fresh fish, chalk board over the bar said, *Catch of the Day: Lasagne*. Alice's Michael said,' adopting an accent, 'And what kind of a net would you be using to catch that?'

Duncan saying, 'Is that a post-modern Irish accent?' Then: 'Sounds like a real Irish pub, though.'

Carol saying, 'You're contradicting yourself there, somewhere.'

Duncan more concerned that he had fallen into the racial stereotype... years of conditioning, you dropped your guard for just one moment.

The Irish as thick bastards.

Angry with himself.

Carol saying, 'No, seriously, what you said about the theme pub is exactly it... the pub is Irish, but not Irish... it's a virtual Irish.'

'And you're not supposed to know the difference?'

'Of course you are, otherwise it wouldn't be post modern.'

District Line train crossing the railway bridge, heading towards Richmond. The water starting to move back downriver, the swans turning, holding their own against the current. Duncan, his glass empty, wondering if he should suggest another, wondering if he could say, 'Let's go on from here, have dinner, somewhere...'

Instead, checking his watch, saying, 'It's getting on, Lindsay will be wondering where I've got to.'

Carol laughing.

Saying, 'She might think you're with another woman.'

What did that mean?

Did it mean anything?

Carol saying, 'I know this is personal, don't answer if you don't want to, but have you ever been unfaithful to Lindsay?'

The two of them standing, now, Duncan wishing that he had made a move, any move, covered her hand with his while they were sitting at the table...

Talking.

Still not asking her to dinner.
Saying, 'I can't say the thought has never been there.'

6

Kiren on top now, wearing the black chenille jumper, nothing else, she had put it on to go for a pee. Darren inside her, neither of them moving, both teasing, Darren saying, 'I never felt this big with other women,' reaching up, both hands, her pear-shaped titties warm beneath the fabric, each pointing away from the other as if neither of them could bear to face the competition, Kiren, that lazy smile on her face, saying, 'My very own bit of rough.'

Trying for Darren's west London accent.

The 'bit of' pronounced 'bitta'.

As in pitta.

The bread.

Darren saying, 'It's the T-s you come unstuck on, try it again, don't let your tongue touch the roof of your mouth.' Then saying, 'Pint of bitter,' swallowing the T-s, the 'bitter' coming out as *bit her*, but no gap. Darren saying, 'There's an H in there somewhere, after the T-s.'

Kiren saying, 'You moved.'

Darren saying, 'No way.'

Kiren saying, 'Say my favourite.'

'What?'

'You know... town hall.'

'Town hall?'

Coming out as *tunnel*.

Kiren laughing.

The laughter touching Darren down there.

A vibration.

Darren saying, 'Now, you moved.'

'I did not.'

Then, Kiren saying, 'Make me laugh, again… it feels good.'

'That counts as moving.'

'Does not.'

'I don't think I could take it.'

'I'm going to win, you know that?'

'In your dreams.'

Darren thinking about anything… cricket, pigeon shit on the paintwork of the Jaguar, the Queen Mother waving… Kiren leaning forward, her hair brushing his face, whispering, 'Angel-Face', the name she called him when they were in bed, saying, that first time they met, Zoë's twenty-fourth, her parents had hired the function room at the Thameside Health Club, 'It's so unfair… any woman would die for eye-lashes like that.'

Happy birthday, Zoë.

Weekend for two in Paris… only, you're going to have to take somebody else.

Zoë and Kiren supposed to be such good friends.

So much for sisterhood.

Darren at the bar, not sure at first if she was taking the piss, saying, 'What can I get you?'

Kiren saying, 'Out of here.'

Then saying, 'It's still warm.'

Meaning the bonnet of the car.

Outside, in the club car-park, skirt hiked up round her waist, backside pressed into the paintwork of the Jaguar, one leg over the front wing, shoe falling off… Darren, his feet slipping on the gravel, trousers catching on the silver mascot, saying, 'Could have done myself a nasty injury.'

Before they got to know each other.

Invented the 'not moving first' game.

Them in the darkness.

Zoë silhouetted in the club-house door.

Crying.

Screaming, 'You shit!'

Darren and Kiren not sure which one of them she meant.

Kiren, now, easing her arms out of the chenille jumper, wrapping the sleeves around her neck, tying a loose knot at the front, like a scarf, saying, 'I want to try it.'

Darren: 'Try what?'
'What you told me Reggie does.'
'I'm not sure about that.'
'Chicken.'
Darren taking the two ends of the scarf, pulling the knot tight.
'Tighter.'
Darren pulling tighter.
'Tighter.'
Darren, not able to help himself, the sleeves as leverage, arching his back into her body.
Kiren, lips curled back.
Low animal groan.
Saying: 'You lose.'

7

Kiren Fleming.
Body to die for... clean teamer, wholesome as a shiny apple, touch of Kiehl's lip-gloss, hint of Jo Malone's linen-scent spray, hair left well alone, pair of Jimmy Choo sandals on her feet she could turn a plain white shirt and a pair of black trousers into a style statement. No spirulina, vitamin B-supplements, special diets...Kiren threw up one time she tried Ayurvedic tea... no gym sessions pencilled in the diary, weights, Stairmaster, cycling, rowing.

Daily shower.
Hair tonic.
One part cider vinegar to four parts water.
Body oil.
That's all it took.
Kiren Fleming was a natural...

Dropped names like APC, Jil Sander, Calvin Klein; said things like, 'That's on the bus,' because it was a buzz phrase in New York. Her world falling apart – that's how she put it to Darren – when her mother, late in life, read too much Greer and Millet, listened too much to what Anita Roddick had to say about dwindling world resources, left her father, Air-Vice Marshal James Arthur Fleming (retired) fighter ace in World War Two under Douglas Bader, 242 Squadron, part of Leigh Mallory's Big Wing, moved to a terraced house in Islington, took Kiren out of private school in Winchester, sent her to the local comprehensive... her mother immersing herself in good causes, wire sculptures made by political prisoners from Mozambique on the mantlepiece, needing to make up for all those years of privilege.

Kiren saying, 'But, *I* haven't had all those bloody years of privilege.'

Her mother saying, 'You've had enough… and don't swear in front of your mother, there's a sweety '

Kiren screaming, 'N1… that's almost…' hardly able to say the word, '…Hackney!'

Local kids from the housing estate across the road firing slug guns at her mother's VW Camper, refugees staying in the house, 'Just for a few nights, dear,' meaning months, her mother's *coq au pineau* so right-on you had to pick the feathers out.

Kiren out of there at eighteen, passed her GNBQ in Tourism and Leisure, her father, now a prominent local Tory Party activist, still living at Windcroft, ten bedroom mock-Tudor in four acres, a heart-shaped pool added by the previous owner, something in PR in the Sixties… 'Water leisure installation,' Kiren's first steady had called it, an estate agent, dumped him when he started hearing wedding bells… Daddy still living alone, housekeeper in three times a week, never remarried.

Said Kiren could move back in any time she wanted.

Berkshire.

The Rotary Club dinner and dance…

Who needed it?

Her mother in Rwanda, now, helping with the repatriation of Hutu refugees returning from Zaire, saying over the telephone, 'God knows what will happen to the rest of them if Kabila kicks Mobutu out.' Kiren, not much idea what her mother was talking about, saying, 'Mother, don't you think you're getting a little too old for this kind of thing?'

Her mother saying, 'There's only two hotels in Burundi worthy of the name… hot running water, that kind of thing… one of them's an Inter-Continental… and a taxi from the airport is *not* a good idea.'

Needless to say, she was staying at neither of the hotels she had recommended.

'Why don't you come over… there's a lot you could do?'

'Mother, you finally developed a sense of humour.'

Dotty before she left home.

Dorothy, after she moved them to Islington.

Should have been the other way around.

Kiren set up in a ground floor flat in Westbourne Park Road, all the bills, rent, electricity, gas, water, telephone paid for through her father's account with Coutt's. The flat, all white walls, varnished wood floors, giant-sized cream crockery... one room, a row of striped beach-huts, red, blue, grey, against the wall, nursery wardrobes from Conran's in Kensington. Kiren kept all her clothes in them, had loved the beach-huts at first sight.

Why she should have been wandering around the children's department at Conran's...

God only knows.

Ten o'clock Wednesday morning, Helen, who lived in the basement flat, regular and exclusive clientele, took American Express, catching Kiren at the front door in her dressing gown, seeing the red burn marks, the red scabs forming on her neck, saying, 'That only works for men.'

Then: 'Kiren, I never saw you as that kind of girl.'

Kiren saying, 'What kind of girl?'

Then: 'What kind of girl am I, Helen, you tell me?'

Bursting into tears there on the doorstep, litre carton of fresh-squeezed orange juice in one hand, pint of milk on the step by her feet.

8

Stoney, on one as usual, saying, 'Imagine, halfway through the film… good guy says, "You'd better do me now, while you've still got the chance," bad guy says, "Sounds reasonable," blows the good guy's head clean off his fucking shoulders.'

Kevin: 'Then, there wouldn't be any more film, would there, you daft twat.'

Stoney: 'What about… His girlfriend comes along, avenges him. Demi Moore or Sharon Stone would be perfect. Women's power, it's all the go, now.'

Kevin singing: *'If you wanna be my lover…'*

Spice Girls.

Dennis saying to Stoney, 'Your Grace, for example?'

Stoney saying, 'Don't fucking talk to me about Grace.'

Darren thinking: Three wise monkeys.

See nothing, hear nothing, know nothing.

Why?

Because they were ignorant as shit, that's why.

Saying to Dennis, already brought up the business with Reggie, no names, mind you, 'You're not interested, Dennis, just say the word.'

Dennis saying, 'I'll think about it, right?'

Darren nursing his second large scotch, that would have to be it if he didn't want to get nicked, wondering why he bothered, stuck in the Mason's Arms, arse-end of Acton, Stoney saying to Darren, earlier, after he had fixed him up with the glazing job, 32 Belvedere, 'How come you knew to find us in here?'

Fucking stroll-on!

'It didn't take a genius, Stoney.'

Then: 'I spoke to Grace, she said, if I was to see you, to tell you to go fuck yourself… you two had a bit or a falling out, I gather.'

Kevin saying, 'Sore point, Darren.'

Stoney: 'Lay off, will you?'

Darren thinking, He was going to have Dennis before the night was out.

Teach him what for…

No uncertain terms.

Kevin saying, now, 'Or that bird in the Alien films… what was her name?'

Stoney: 'Signourney Weaver.'

'It's without the N, Stoney.'

'Sigourey?'

'No, you daft twat. Anyway, she's too old.'

'I wouldn't say no…'

Dennis saying, 'That don't mean a lot, Stoney…'

'…did you see her in that one about the apes?'

'Gorillas.'

'Same difference… with that Australian bloke in the car ads on the telly, he was in that film with Tom Cruise, the one with the two of them juggling glasses, mixing up cocktails. Imagine Ted doing that, spinning your bottle of Carlsberg Export over his shoulder, pouring it behind his back,' looking towards the bar, laughing.

Kevin saying, 'Fat chance of that.'

Ted at the far end of the bar reading the *Standard*.

Another busy night in the Mason's.

Darren wanting today over with.

Dead and buried…

This afternoon with the bank manager, Oliver-fucking-Holland, sat there in his office with his shirt sleeves rolled up, casual approach, saying to Darren, 'Without substantial collateral, I don't see how it will be possible.'

Smug little bastard.

Darren had made it through the personal accounts manager, the small business adviser, everybody clocking an ear to his business, just to hear this crap. Saying, 'I was hoping my track record might mean something.'

'Well, of course, we do take that into account.'

Then: 'I understand you've now sold your lease on the premises?'

'Cost cutting exercise... getting rid of the dead wood. You can understand that.'

Sold the lease to Eddie, his shop manager, only nine months to run, stupid git.

Told him he could use the name.

No extra cost.

Glass Act.

Glass as in 'Class'.

So, what was original these days?

Oliver-fucking-Holland saying, 'On these figures,' tarted up by Alison, 'perhaps we should review the situation in, say, twelve months?'

'Twelve months?'

Thinking, wanting to say, When was it they stopped stoning money-lenders out of the village? How come you lot got to be so fucking respectable?

Oliver-fucking-Holland saying, 'Your account has not been in good order for the past few months, Mr Friend.' Treating Darren like some school kid, up before the headmaster. Remembering the good old days, previous bank manager, Darren would just knock on the door, waltz right in... it was all, 'Cliff, you spare a moment?' 'Darren, good to see you,' coming round from behind the desk, limp handshake.

Like grabbing hold of a dead lizard.

Saying to Stoney, now, 'Anyway, she's a dyke.'

Kevin saying, 'Sigourney Weaver? How do you know that?'

Darren not answering.

Dennis waiting for Darren to get back to the business with Reggie.

Playing hard to get...

Dennis Frost, Kevin's older brother, three years difference, 'Frosty' when they were back at school, very handy in a spot of trouble... now, look at him, sad toss-pot. Pushing thirty, fuck all to show for it, just coming to realise he never would have...

Dennis Frost, this is your life.

Darren needing to acquaint him with the change in pecking order, wondering if he was going to do him in the pub, or outside... what the fuck, it wasn't his local.

Stoney saying, 'Takes you back, this, us all sat round having a drink. Just like the old days.'

Darren thinking, Must be a fucking mind reader.

Dennis saying, 'I'll burst into tears in a minute.'

'You know, gives you a sense of asha-dejar.'

What Stoney always said.

When he meant 'Déjà vu.'

Kevin saying, 'Sounds like a horse, might have won the National.'

Dennis saying, 'Déjà vu, you tit-head.'

Than, to Darren, 'How's the new squeeze?'

'Out of your league, Dennis.'

The pot man coming across to clear the table. Dad's Army, they called him... spitting image of the one who looked old but wasn't, not then, anyway.

Dad's Army saying, 'Done with this lot, have you?'

Darren thinking, If only.

Dennis saying, 'Yours, too, from what I hear... coming across, is she?'

Darren on his feet.

Chair falling over backwards.

His hand reaching full span, feeling the solid weight of the glass ash tray, lifting the ash tray, one handed, the way a goalkeeper or a basketball player would lift a ball.

Starting his swing.

Glasses going over.

Mobile ringing in Darren's jacket pocket.

Dad's Army saying, 'I hate those bloody things... shouldn't be allowed in a pub.'

Dennis, arms up to protect his face, Darren with the phone to his ear, Kiren, on the other end, saying, 'Angel Face? Where have you been all my life?'

PART TWO
A Good Seeing To...

Lying in bed on his left side in the darkness, Frank Cannon was wondering if it was all worth the effort any more... legs drawn up to his stomach, back bent, like he was a baby in his cot ninety-one years ago, except, then he would have had his thumb stuck in his mouth, not his hands between his legs nursing his cock. Both his hands useless, like bent claws, as if they had been sewn together at the finger-tips, knees swollen with pain, Frank deciding that it had got to the point when he had had enough. The doctors telling him that, apart from the rheumatoid arthritis, for his age, he was a remarkably healthy man.

Could go on for years like this.
Couldn't imagine anything worse.
Going on for years like this.
Frank Cannon had lived in the ground floor flat, 17 Mulberry Close, near The Butts, Brentford, for close on forty years, the last fourteen of those years alone, since his wife, Esther, had passed on... all those months up and down the hospital, day in, day out, radio-therapy, chemotherapy.

Doctors.
What did they know?
His son, David, living in Toronto, Esther already too ill to get out there for the wedding, three grandchildren he had never seen, card at Christmas, if he was lucky, signed by the both of them. Petra, David's wife, his daughter-in-law, always adding a note: 'Definitely be across this year... that's a promise...
'Lots of love.'
District nurse, meals on wheels, home help... the district nurse coming in twice a day, let herself in at eight thirty every morning, saying, 'And how are we today, Frank?' Got him onto the bedside commode, washed, shaved, dressed, out into the sitting room in the wheel-chair – couldn't manage the Zimmer any more – lifted him into the armchair, switched on the television. Bottle tucked into the side of the armchair for when he was taken short, Frank stuck there all day till she came back in the evening, put him back to bed.
What kind of life was that?
Frank thinking.
I ask you?
Used to be a fit man, strong as a horse, played football, cricket,

knew how to look after himself, too, when he had to... Frank Cannon had never walked away from a fight in his life. All his mates dead, now... worked as a fitter on the buses, London Transport Depot at Gunnersbury, knocked it all down a few years back, Trafalgar Development, still hadn't put anything up in its place, last he heard. Christ, he had seen some changes in his lifetime!

Now, all these yuppy couples moving in up and down the street.

Au pairs.

Foreign cars.

Loud voices... like they thought everybody should want to know their business.

Old Mrs Riggs, lived on the corner, she was loud enough, but she couldn't have held a candle to this lot. Frank could remember when it was all market people lived round here, Brentford Market, wholesale fruit and vegetables, at the foot of Kew Bridge, the Express, on the junction, open all night.

Fights round the back.

When there were differences needed settling.

Frank smiling in the darkness, the first time he had done that since he could remember... the young couple who had moved in next door, the husband knocking 'to discuss' the tree. Frank saying to him, 'I'll give you "discuss the tree". You wanted a back garden without a tree next door you should have bloody moved somewhere else.'

Would have landed him one, too.

Little toss-pot wasn't worth it.

Aware of the drip of water on to his bed-clothes.

The bed soaked.

The flat upstairs empty since the new landlords took over, Sterling Realty, home-help sent them off a postal order for the rent every fortnight. Builders in, the last couple of days, banging about over his head... must be something to do with them.

Frank Cannon turning painfully in the bed, his clawed hands reaching either side of the bedside-lamp to squeeze the switch unit, turn the light on.

Seeing the bulge in the plaster.

Had to be a ton of water up there, waiting to come down on him.

Trying to sit upright on the edge of the bed.

Toppling falling to the floor.

Between the bed and the dressing table.

Unable to move.
Cold.
Wet.
Thinking, Bleedin' hell… how long am I supposed to lie here like this for?

9

Stoney Todd had always preferred hanging around with kids who were a lot younger than him, joining in their games of football over Gunnersbury Park, them much smaller than him, being able to order them about, get more than his fair share of the ball… not like how it was with blokes his own age. That's how he had come to get to know the Frost brothers, Dennis and Kevin, Kevin still at Twyeford Secondary, before he got kicked out in his last year, caught shagging a second year, broad daylight, in Northfields Park, by one of the teachers on her way home. Kevin, being Kevin, swore he didn't know she was under-age, despite she was in school uniform – blue blazer, white socks, note from her mother in her shoulder bag excusing her from games… time of month.

Forged signature.

Kevin, himself, only fifteen the week before.

Their mother, Mrs Frost – Pat – had given Kevin a Ninja T-shirt, Rafael, thought he would be pleased, how much did she know?

Fifteen.

A Ninja T-shirt.

Kevin saying, when she gave it to him: 'Gross… or what?'

Which is exactly how many of them Pat Frost's boyfriend had to get rid of now the turtle craze had peaked… one more loser in a long line of losers their mother seemed to attract. Dennis saw him off one Friday night, the boyfriend coming round pissed after the pubs had shut, only hit her the once before Dennis, eighteen then, broke his nose…

Then his right arm.

In two places.

The Frost brothers.

Kevin, Jack the Rabbit straight out of the starting gate. Two children by Michelle by the time he was nineteen, divorced at twenty-one. His mother, Pat, saying, when she heard about the break up, 'You can't say I didn't warn you....should stick with your own kind, isn't that what I said?'

Michelle's parents Jamaican.

Michelle a Londoner.

Born and bred.

Now, Monica with one in the oven, Stoney saying to her last night, bed made up on the sofa, Kevin and Stoney saying nothing about what happened between Dennis and Darren, 'What do you want, then... a boy or a girl?'

Trying to be friendly.

Monica saying, 'What I want most of all, Stoney, is you out of my fucking house.'

And Dennis, still living at home with his mother in Prescott Gardens, swore he only stayed to protect her from herself... best man at Stoney's wedding to Grace, sorted out the barman at the reception when he started charging before the bar limit was reached, dragging him over the bar by his collar, saying, 'I don't want to be creating a disturbance at my best mate's wedding.'

Stoney loved that.

The idea that he was Dennis Frost's best mate.

Kevin there, too; in his best suit, just started up with Monica, the two of them all lovey-dovey, couldn't keep their hands off each other, Kevin amazed that Stoney had managed to pull a bird, any bird, let alone a bird like Grace.

Stoney telling Dennis and Kevin about Grace, this was months before the wedding, how he met her down the Powell Road, Stoney was in to collect his gyro, Grace in one of the interview cubicles giving somebody what for, you could have heard her all the way to Chiswick Roundabout, telling them where they could stick their availability for work, pissed as a newt... just heard about her old man and the twenty-seven thousand six hundred he had left her. Stoney, for once in his life, in the right place at the right time, helped her up off the floor when she fell flat on her face on the way out, the two of them going on a bender that lasted six days.

Kevin saying, 'I don't know what she sees in you, Stoney, could be a tasty looking bird, she looked after herself a bit better.'

Dennis saying, 'Amount she drinks, probably thinks there's two of him... thinks she's shagging two blokes at the same time.'

Then, Kevin: 'Stoney with two knobs, and I bet he has no idea what to do with either one of them.'

The two of them laughing.

McDonald's, in Acton High Road.

Stoney not caring what they said.

They were his mates.

Never called him 'retard' like all the other blokes used to before Dennis was around.

Never made any of those other insinuations about him and young kids...

Filthy-minded bastards.

Stoney watching the late night film, Channel Four, on Kevin and Monica's front-room sofa, the one with Richard Gere as the bent cop, couldn't remember what it was called... seen it before, though, probably on video from Blockbuster. That woman from *Roseanne* was in it, Roseanne's sister, the neurotic one, up to the bit where Richard Gere shoots her. Stoney wondering what it felt like to get shot.

How much it hurt.

The other cop, Godfather Three, Andy Garcia, not sure if Richard Gere is screwing his wife or not, big fight scene in the good cop's bedroom, Richard Gere, full of bullet holes, lying on the bedroom floor, his last words to the good cop, 'Fucking yuppy.'

Stoney liked that.

'Fucking yuppy.'

Just like Darren Friend with his flash car, his flash bird, and his mobile... forgetting where it was he came from, always used to be hanging around with them. Thinking about what had happened between Dennis and Darren in the Mason's. Surprised that Dennis had taken it lying down like he did, asking Dennis, after Darren was gone, what he was going to do about it? If he needed any help, just say the word, Stoney was up for it.

The least he could do.

Dennis being his best mate.

Dennis saying, 'Let it rest, for fuck's sake, Stoney, will you!'

Then, thinking about Grace.

Holding himself, smiling in the dark... just the one knob, contrary to all the joking. Wondering if they could hear him from upstairs like he heard them, Kevin and Monica going at it hammer and tongs just as soon as they were up there, Monica five months gone, too, and starting to show. Stoney having a laugh to himself, an old *Avengers* re-run now on the TV, Diana Rigg looking very sexy in her black leotard, thinking his right hand was hardly likely to start screaming, 'Oh, Kevin! Oh, Kevin! Oh, Kevin!' once he got to the vinegar strokes, now was it?

Remembering how Grace had shown him *exactly* what to do with it...

Only, he was not about to tell Dennis and Kevin any of that.

Not ever.

Some things are private.

Even from your best mates.

10

The first person Darren Friend ever really hurt, hospital hurt, was – funnily enough – his old man. There at the kitchen sink in Glenthorne Road having a glass of water so he wouldn't feel like shit when he woke up. Darren, fourteen years old, going through his punk phase. Spiked hair, bleached blonde, bondage collar, leather coat... this was before he started hanging around with Dennis and Kevin, and that fuckwit, Stoney, went Two-Tone with Fred Perry tennis tops, stay-press trousers or tonics, loafers instead of Doc Martens... tidied himself up a bit. Feeling like a king – not *The King*, he hadn't got into him, yet – just shagged Samantha Mitchell, his old man saying, 'Look at you... what *do* you think you look like?'

Standing behind Darren in his dressing gown.

Six-thirty in the morning.

Darren, holding the glass up to his mouth, could smell Samantha Mitchell on his fingers.

The old man saying, 'You're not so old I can't still fetch you one, you know that, don't you?' Darren well up, thinking about Samantha Mitchell, how her eyes had rolled up in her head, started howling, Darren, thinking she might be having a fit, saying, 'You all right?' Then: 'Am I hurting you?' Samantha biting down on her bottom lip, going, 'Don't stop, Darren... please, don't stop.' Back seat of her boyfriend's Ford Sierra, furry dice, raised back suspension, fish-tail exhaust, the full cowboy works. The Sierra parked down the road from the party, Cunningham Street, Shepherd's Bush, Zippy inside, out of his head on whiz and Red Bull, pogo-ing to The Damned, the whole party could have been shagging his bird, Zippy wouldn't have noticed.

The old man saying, 'What time of the morning do you call this? It's not a bloody hotel me and your mother are running, here, you know.'

This, two years after the old man had lost the job with Cherry Blossom, accounts department, the first to go when they brought in computerisation. Pissed ever since, his old lady the only bread-winner, check-out operator at Sainsbury's, taking all the overtime she could get, even after she got the promotion to customer services supervisor.

Four years before the old man did the world a big favour.

Bottle of scotch a day, liver finally giving out on him.

Sclerosis.

His old lady up there with him at Charing Cross when he sat up in the hospital bed, ward full of visitors, vomited blood all over her.

Gave up the ghost, there and then.

Good fucking riddance, as far as Darren was concerned.

Darren, there at the sink, saying, 'Why don't you get off my fucking back?'

Had just shagged Samantha Mitchell.

Had wanted to shag Samantha Mitchell ever since he first clapped eyes on her, her with Zippy down The Clarendon, Hammersmith Broadway, before they knocked the whole lot down, built a new shopping mall and bus garage. Zippy, nineteen and full of himself, next stop, stadium tour of the States, roadying for some band doing the support. Three blokes and a bird singer, couldn't play a note between them, thought they were too charismatic to need bother with shit like that… bunch of absolute no-hopers, like Zippy. Darren, amazed Zippy had been able to pull something that tasty, saying to her, in the bathroom at the party, her bent over the bath, fishing around in the ice for a bottle of Pils, her tight little backside looking gorgeous in a pair of black 501s, 'Thought I recognised that face… Samantha, isn't it?'

Samantha straightening up, turning around to give him her best drop-dead expression, Darren taking the bottle of Pils from her, flicking the metal cap off with his Bic disposable, saying, 'Neat, huh?'

Handing back the bottle.

Samantha saying, 'Actually, it's Sam. I don't like Samantha, makes me sound like some tarty debutante.'

'Or, that page three girl with the gynormous boobs.'

'Chance would be a fine thing.'

Darren making a point of looking.

Samantha…

Sam… wearing a leopard-skin shirt-top, cuffs rolled up, top three buttons undone, looked like she had found it in some Oxfam Shop.

Darren saying, 'They're not so bad.'

Samantha, ultra-cool, not like most birds when you took it all in like that.

Darren saying, 'If it's all the same with you, I'd just as soon stick with Samantha… when we get to shagging on a regular basis, I start groaning "Sam" every time I come, other birds might take me for a poofta.'

Giving her the big grin.

Samantha saying, 'You're Darren. In Kate's class, aren't you?'

Kate, her younger sister by four years.

'Only, because I'm intellectually challenged. Been stuck in that class for years, now.'

Samantha lighting a Benson… blowing the smoke up towards the ceiling, 'I am the anti-Christ', Johnny Rotten, starting up in the other room. Darren saying, 'So, how would you like to fuck a retard?'

Samantha saying, 'Beats cradle-snatching.'

Darren's old man, behind him at the sink, saying, 'If you think for one moment…'

Fourteen years ago.

And that wasn't the last of it, either.

Him and Samantha at it behind Zippy's back for months.

Any time.

Any place.

Then, one night, outside The Electric Cinema, Darren giving Samantha a quick squeeze even Zippy couldn't fail to notice, Darren forced to kick all kinds of shit out of the daft git. Zippy with back problems from that night on, lost his job with the band, who needs a roady can't hump gear? Darren thinking he probably did the fuck-wit a favour. Samantha, though, went weird on him. Wouldn't even give him the time of day, after that night.

Birds.

Who could fathom what goes on in their tiny little minds?

Darren running the tap, pouring himself another glass of water, his old man: '... I'm not going to put up with that kind of gutter language...'

Samantha and Zippy ended up married... no accounting for taste. Darren last saw her about three years back, must have had her two kids in school by then, working as a cashier for the Halifax Building Society, one of their up-town branches, off Haymarket. Waited in the queue at her counter just for a laugh. When he got to the front, big grin on his face, the same big grin she could never bring herself to say 'no' to, Darren saying, 'I'd like to make a withdrawal.'

Samantha, cool as a cucumber, had to give her that, saying, 'And your account number?'

Fingers poised over her terminal.

Like they were perfect strangers.

Darren saying, 'Samantha... let me take you away from this humdrum existence you've landed yourself in.'

Samantha leaning forward, face almost touching the re-enforced perspex, mouth level with the circle of little round holes you spoke through, saying, 'Come closer.

'Closer.

'Closer.'

Then, Darren with his face pressed up against the perspex, Samantha whispering, 'Fuck off, you psychotic dick-breath.'

Darren, going out through the revolving doors, thinking:

Tragic waste.

The old man: '...under my own roof!'

Darren saying, 'Your roof? I don't recall you paying many of the bills round here, lately.'

Remembering his old lady saying, seemed like it got to be every night once the old man lost his job, 'Better keep out of your father's way, dear... he's not in the best of moods.'

Meaning, he was blind pissed.

About to bust Darren round the head.

No matter what he did or said.
The old man saying, 'What did you just say to me?'
Darren saying, 'You heard, toss-pot.'
Deciding, Why the fuck not?
Grabbing the old man by the hair, banging his face down on the top of the fridge.
Once.
Twice.
Three times.
Darren never feeling this good in his whole life.
Not even earlier.
When he was shagging Samantha Mitchell.

11

First there had been the pick-up in Ellesmere Road, the woman still in her dressing gown at eleven o'clock, offering him a cup of tea after he had got the Zanussi out to the van... rubbing her fat thighs against his leg as she leaned over him at the kitchen table to pour the tea, brushing her tit against his ear, saying, 'Help yourself to the biscuits, I've plenty more in the cupboard.'

Daft slag.

Then, Eric, on the mobile just as soon as he was away from there, heading back to the shop, saying, 'Where the fuck are you? I've got an empty workshop here, Shane with nothing to occupy his tiny mind but the *Mirror* crossword.'

Dennis wanting to throw up.

Could still smell the woman's arm-pits from when she lent over him.

Transit window wound right down. Despite it was pissing with rain. Saying to Eric, 'I'm on my way.'

Wondering if there had been an exact moment in time when he had stopped being Dennis Frost...

The Dennis Frost.

Frosty.

Knowing that at some point, somewhere down the years between the Twyeford days and now, he had lost it...

The power.

The respect.

Everything moves on... now, it was all down to money, Dennis could see that, and, as far as making any real money was concerned, Dennis was fucking hopeless. Forget the likes of Darren-fucking-Friend – even his brother, young Kevin, was pulling in more than him now, fixing up motors with Dave Cullen up under the arches down by Stamford Brook, enough in the kitty to look after his ex, Michelle, and the two kids, and plenty left over for him and Monica to have a sit-down Chinese or Indian any time they felt like it...

Legit, too.

If you could believe Dave and Kevin.

Even Stoney, fucking half-wit that he was, on benefit, dossing out with Kevin and Monica, was worth more than Dennis.

The house in Pope's Lane.

All paid up.

Half of it his.

Dennis running an amber coming out of Windmill Road. Suit in a black Beamer forced to brake, the driver leaning on his horn. Dennis pulling up across his path, head out of the Transit window, saying, 'You got a problem, we can pull over, sort it out.' The driver of the Beamer shouting, 'Oh, grow up, will you?' reversing, then driving around the Transit, giving Dennis the finger as he went past. Dennis moving off as other drivers started on their horns.

Grow up?

Dennis thinking, 'What the fuck.'

Marking time – just till the right thing came along.

His job with White Goods – it wasn't called that when he went there at sixteen, straight from school, just plain Dunlop's... washing machine repairs, overhauls and maintenance, shop front between Hair by Allan and Hot Snaps on Northfield Avenue. Eric, Frank Dunlop's son, had come up with the new name after Frank retired, moved down to Pagham with his wife, Lily. 'White Goods?' Dennis had said when Eric told him the new name. 'Got to move with the times,' Eric had said, leaving Dennis none the wiser. Eric Dunlop had been one of the kids Dennis used to scare shitless back when they were at school.

Now look at him.

Poncing around in his four-wheel drive.

Couldn't even get that right.

Vauxhall Frontera.

Like Kevin said, when he heard: 'Useless pile of shit.'

Dennis not sure, at first, if Kevin meant Eric or the Frontera.

Frank Dunlop had started Dennis off driving the van, him and Eric doing all the lifting and carrying between them, Frank, when there was a quiet moment, teaching them the ins and outs of washing machine maintenance... pulley systems, drive belts, electrics, water pumps, plumbing in. Nowadays, with every thing electronic, any half-wit with a service manual could have a washing machine back up and running in the time it took to change a modem. Which was about the extent of what Eric's mate, Shane, did back at the workshop all day.

Leaving Dennis to drive the van.

Pick-ups and deliveries.

Thirty years old...

Still driving the fucking van.

His mother, Pat, saving, 'It's a good honest living. Nothing to be ashamed of in being a van driver ' Dennis wondering what the fuck made her such an expert on good honest livings; low-life she was always dragging home with her from the pub. And the old man... Dennis could just about remember him, string vest, there at the kitchen sink washing himself, Kevin still in his buggy when the fucker walked out of the door one morning, never came back.

'Good riddance to bad rubbish,' Pat saying.

Dennis knowing she missed him.

More than she would admit.

Kept the wedding photograph on the mantlepiece in her bedroom, her looking very sixties in her mini-skirt and long straight hair, the old man, hair covering his ears, double-breasted suit with flair trousers... evil looking bastard. Everybody on his mother's side of the family said that Dennis looked like his old man, took after him too... but Dennis was having none of that.

As for Kevin.

He didn't look like either of them.

Not one bit.

Dennis and Kevin having a laugh about it, saying maybe that was what it was all about, the break-up, why the old man did a runner... Kevin, the result of a bit of lust between their mother and the milkman. Afternoon delights with the man from the Prudential.

Some shit like that.

The way she had carried on since the old man left, wouldn't have surprised either of them. It would have gone a long way, too, in explaining the differences between Dennis and Kevin, people always surprised when they found out they were brothers... like, for example, the way they were with women. Kevin always at it – like bees to the honey they were with him, and Kevin never yet learned to say 'no'. Dennis, well, he had gone steady with Elaine for a couple of years, after they left Twyeford, planned to marry once Dennis was earning enough, the two of them saving for a deposit on a decent house, Elaine working as a shop assistant in Boots, the Ealing Broadway Branch. Which was where she met the pharmaceutical rep, house out near Watford, company car – Ford Mondeo – good salary, plus performance bonus... first thing Dennis knew what was going on, Elaine was up the club, despite the two of them deciding they would wait.

Elaine's parents being RC.

Dennis not caring, much, either way.

Dennis would never forget the look on Elaine's face when he said, 'Pregnant... how?'

Before he gave her one.

Like he was the thickest bastard ever walked this planet.

Kevin saying, when Dennis told him, 'If you want, we can break the geezer's legs.'

Dennis – perhaps that was the moment it started, when he ceased to be *the* Dennis Frost...

'Frosty.'

Lost the power.

The respect.

Saying to Kevin, 'Kevin, she's not worth the aggravation.'

Kevin knowing that wasn't the point.

Giving Dennis a look.

The same look Stoney gave him in the Mason's Arms after the fracas with Darren Friend.

Dennis parking up the Transit van on the double yellow out front of the shop, seeing Eric looking out of the window, standing by the till, then coming out through the door, across the pavement, saying to Dennis, 'Where the fuck you been all morning?'

A couple of old dears with shopping bags tut-tutting at Eric's language.

Dennis thinking: Eric Dunlop talking to him, Dennis Frost, like that.

Knowing he was going to ring Darren.

Swallow it.

Whatever it took, so he could give give Eric-fucking-Dunlop a salutary reminder...

Why he used to scare him shitless.

Saying to Eric, 'Don't take it out on me, Eric. You can blame that fucking bitch on Ellesmere. On heat, she was...

'Wouldn't take no for an answer.'

Eric, laughing, saying, 'You're going to come up with an excuse, at least make it believable.'

12

On the drive over to Reggie Crystal's for dinner, half an hour late because Kiren couldn't decide between the seamed stretch-cotton vest from the boy's department, Marks & Sparks, or the Pinks white button-up shirt – finally deciding on the shirt, tail out – Darren was telling her how it was Reggie had come up with his original 'fuck off' money.

'He embezzled his own *mother*?'

'You used that word, not me.'

'Darren, fraud is fraud.'

'After all, she was his mother, probably would have let him have the money, anyway, if he'd asked nicely.'

'I don't think that's the point.'

Checking out her hair.

Vanity mirror, back of the sun-visor.

Five minutes drive from Kiren's place to Stanley Crescent, Kiren had wanted to walk, Darren not happy with the idea, walking back late, who knows what kind of psychos you were likely to bump into, especially with Kiren putting it out like she was?

'We could take a cab.'

Darren grateful that she had given up calling them Floppies. Floppy?

How the fuck did you get 'floppy' from minicab?

Saying: 'I'll drive.'

Telling her about Reggie's trip out to Barcelona in the spring of '82 armed with his mother's power of attorney, authorisation as sole signatory on all her accounts, found a local solicitor, Antonio Herez, who knew exactly what was required of him, came to a deal with the property developers on the flat his mother owned in the apartment block, Placa Reial, prime acreage, city centre, the developers wanted to knock down the whole block, build a shopping mall.

The final deal involving a substantial lump sum. Plus a small annual percentage on ground rental.

Reggie's mother dead ten years, now, pulmonary pneumonia, aged ninety-two. During the last few years of her life she used to get confused, kept ringing Reggie up, asking him what the time was... whenever she asked about Spain, Reggie would bung her a couple of hundred, say, 'Currency restrictions, very difficult getting the cash out of the country... any time you want to fly out there, take a holiday, wouldn't cost you a penny.'

Zimmer.

Stenna stair lift.

Who was Reggie kidding?

Take a holiday?

Kiren saying, 'Just how much are we talking about?'

'Up to the time of her death? Reggie reckons about three-quarters of a million.'

'Three quarters of a million? He steals three quarters of a million from his own mother?'

Then: '*And* he likes to hang from ceilings?'

'That's Reggie.

'I can't wait to meet him.'

Darren holding back the part about the solicitor, Antonio Herez, cutting himself in on the action, Reggie, having to fly out there, pick up Herez's young daughter from school, take her round to her Daddy's office, break her finger.

Saying to Herez, 'The message is very simple, right?'

Herez holding his daughter in his arms.

Nodding his head...

In agreement.

Kiren saying, 'He sounds dangerous... I like dangerous men.'

Darren saying, 'Kiren, you don't know the half.'

13

When Kevin popped round Michelle's place to drop off some money for her and the kids, Eric Dunlop's Frontera was parked in the road outside, the two kids were in the front room watching *Heartbreak High* on the box, and Michelle was upstairs in the master bedroom, Eric shagging her senseless on the double-bed, gilt headrest, that Kevin and Michelle had picked out together at Fairdeal Furniture in Southall, not three months before Michelle found out about him and Monica…

Kevin standing in the hall at the top of the stairs, bedroom door pushed open, watching Eric's fat rump pumping up and down, his backside looking especially pallid framed between Michelle's coffee-brown thighs, Michelle going, 'Ah…! Oh…! Ah…!' clinging to Eric's neck, her heels digging into his backside, like he was a horse needed kicking into action.

Kevin, as usual, marvelling at how white the soles of Michelle's feet were…

Compared to the rest of her.

Michelle seeing Kevin over Eric's shoulder.

Saying, 'Well, knock, why don't you?'

Kevin standing there grinning.

Then saying, 'Don't mind me. Do carry on.'

Michelle saying to Eric, 'For fuck's sake, get off me, will you?'

Eric rolling over, sitting up, arms clasped around his knees to hide himself from Kevin. Kevin saying, 'Bit late for modesty, I'd have thought, Eric.'

Eric saying, 'You've no right to come bursting in like this…

you two aren't married any more, or had you forgotten? Michelle can do what she likes.'

'No, I hadn't forgotten. And I haven't forgotten you're a married man yourself, Eric. What would Carol have to say about all this, I wonder?'

Michelle saying, 'You're a fine one to talk.'

Eric swinging his legs off the side of the bed, pulling on his boxer shorts – little pink elephants, would you believe? – standing up to get into his trousers, reaching for his shirt on the back of the bedside chair.

Kevin still looking at Michelle on the bed.

Saying, 'Fucking gorgeous. I'd forgotten just how gorgeous you looked in your all-together.'

Michelle crawling in under the duvet. Sat with it pulled up to her chin.

'Your loss, dick-brain... our breaking up was none of my doing.

'You kicked me out.'

'And what was I supposed to do, you off shagging Monica James every God-given minute of the day.'

'It would have blown over.'

'And I was supposed to wait... catch my own husband on the rebound? Fuck right off, Kevin.'

Eric saying, 'My shoes are downstairs... I'll just get them and be off.'

Talking to no-one in particular.

Kevin, not looking at him, saying, 'Why don't you just do that, Eric.' Waiting till he had left the room, then saying to Michelle, 'Bet you're all of a fluster, me interrupting you and Eric like that?'

Grinning.

Michelle saying, 'You're a cheeky bastard, you know that, don't you, Kevin?'

'It's why you married me.'

'And why I divorced you.'

'Go on, tell me what's going through your head, right this minute.'

Michelle blushing.

Kevin saying, 'You're blushing.'

Remembering that first time he had seen her naked, Kevin saying she had the nicest titties he had ever see – both of them seventeen, just how many titties had Kevin seen at seventeen? – Michelle blushing, Kevin saying, 'I didn't know your lot could do that.'

Michelle saying, 'My lot?'

Could have ended right there...

Kitty and Tatum never been born.

Never existed.

Michelle saying, now, 'You've got a fucking nerve.'

Kevin saying, 'Haven't I just.'

Pushing the bedroom door closed with his foot, only the T-shirt left to take off by the time he reached the bed.

Michelle going, 'Oh, Kevin!'

Kevin, pushing into her, wondering if, when they were through, it would be the right time to bring up her taking on Stoney as a lodger.

Or, maybe, leave it a couple more days.

Couple more fucks.

14

Grace, from the bay window in the upstairs bedroom watched Stoney coming down the garden path, pausing to look at the Cortina Estate up on blocks on the crazy paving, before disappearing beneath the overhang.

Ringing the bell.

Chimes going, *Ding-Dong*.

Brown paper bag in his hand.

Two bottles.

Cutty Sark and Soda Water.

Grace knowing she couldn't let him in, much as she wanted to, those bottles in his hand. Three days, now. Christ, she was trying so hard! Clutching the curtain with her hand, knuckles going white – just like that one time she had flown, package deal to Benedorm, her and Stoney, clutching the arm rests all the way there, all the way back – hearing the bell go *Ding-Dong* again, the sound drifting from room to room, nothing in the whole house moving, not even a tap dripping. Seeing Stoney stepping back from the front door-step, peering into the downstairs front-room window, shielding the daylight from his eyes with a hand, then stepping back some more, looking up to where she was standing

Grace letting the curtain fall back into place.

Standing motionless in the darkness.

Hearing Stoney call, 'Grace?'

Then: 'Grace, it's me. Why don't you open the door. I want to talk to you.'

Stoney Todd.

The nicest, kindest man she could ever have hoped to meet

in her whole life… never raised a hand to her, never raised his voice in anger, even, there on the front doorstep, bottle of scotch whisky in a bag under his arm, calling for her to open the door.

Stoney.

A big baby.

A child.

How would he understand that she couldn't do it – would never make it – with him around?

He'd see what she needed.

Provide it for her…

Short term.

For Stoney Todd, short term was all there was. He would never be able to understand that what she really needed was to go up the fucking wall, screaming and kicking, sobbing and crying, before it was all over.

Grace loving Stoney too much to put him through that.

She was on her own.

The whisky-fuelled row over the house just an excuse.

Who the fuck gave a sod about the house?

A moment Grace had grasped at…

Knowing this was the time.

Now or never.

Wishing she could explain this to Stoney. If only he were like any other man. Laughing.

That was the whole point.

Stoney *wasn't* like any other man.

He cared.

Seeing the two of them on the beach at Broadstairs – they were on one, don't ask how they ended up in Broadstairs – run out of pubs along the front that would serve them, the two of them laughing so much Grace pissed herself, started to cry when she realised what she had done, Stoney hugging her to him, saying, 'But, you're beautiful, you're gorgeous… don't let anybody ever tell you otherwise.'

But, knowing she wasn't beautiful.

She was ugly.

Sordid.

Stinking of stale piss the whole train journey back to London.

A damp patch on the seat when they got off at Charing Cross.

Stoney saying, laughing, 'Wonder where your knickers are by now, probably half-way to France.'

Grace standing in the bay window remembering Stoney, having trouble keeping his balance in the shingle by the water's edge, hurling Grace's knickers out into the waves, seagulls swooping in, hoping for food.

The bell going, *Ding-Dong, Ding-Dong.*

Chimes could never sound urgent.

No matter how many times you pressed the bell.

Lazy sound, drifting around the house.

'Grace! I know you're up there!'

Rattling the letterbox.

'I'm not going away, so you'd better come down, open this door.'

Grace starting to cry in the darkness of the bedroom, imagining how easy, how great it would be... going down to the front door, releasing the latch, the two of them going into the kitchen, finding a couple of clean glasses, ice-cubes from the freezer unit of the fridge, pouring the amber liquid, waiting for that moment when it all went away, just the warmth, the two of them as close as two people could ever get to be...

Before the bottle was empty.

And the phantoms came.

Dancing at the periphery of her vision.

Grace pulling back the curtain, eyes blinded by the sudden daylight, struggling with the window catch, pushing the window open, shouting now, 'Stoney, you fuck off, you hear? You don't go away I'll have the police on to you.'

Stoney carefully placing the brown paper bag on the ground between his feet, spreading his arms, looking up, saying, 'Grace, what are you doing to me? You know I didn't mean it, what I said about the house. It was only talk... let me in, will you?'

Grace shouting down, 'Stoney Todd, you're a greedy, money-grabbing bastard, just like all the rest of them. Now, fuck right off out of my life.'

Knowing it wasn't true.

Not a word of it.

Seeing the tears forming in Stoney's eyes as he looked up at her… tears ready to fall, once he lowered his head.

Slamming the window shut.

Pulling the curtains.

Heavy drapes.

Neither Grace nor Stoney ever wanted morning to come before they were ready.

Grace thinking…

One livener.

Just the one.

Where would the harm be in that?

Not sure how much more of this she could take.

15

Reggie Crystal didn't need to have it confirmed that Ken Lovatt's wife, Daphne, was a sad cow, but there it was… just minutes after they had sat down at the table to eat, Darren and Kiren finally made it, her saying, 'Lovely house, but I'm not sure about the area.'

Reggie doing the honours.

Pouring the chardonnay, saying, 'Do help yourself to the nibbles while Eddy gets fired-up in the kitchen,' the nibbles being spring rolls, prawn and crab butterflies, hot plum sauce with spring onion garnish, then, in response to Daphne's comment, saying, 'I'm not entirely with you?'

Daphne saying, 'Well…'

Darren saying, 'Too many blacks, is what she means… afraid she'll get mugged.'

Kiren saying, 'I don't recall you being so anxious to walk.'

Reggie saying, 'Really, Daphne! You don't want to believe all you read in the *Mail on Sunday*.'

Daphne uncomfortable.

Her husband, Ken, helping himself to a spring roll.

Darren, giving Kiren the look.

Kiren, couldn't care less she had upset Darren, saying, 'Chinese. You can't go far wrong with Chinese, can you?'

Ken Lovatt chiming in, 'Unless you're a vegetarian.'

Kiren saying, 'Are you a vegetarian?'

Ken Lovatt saying, 'Good Lord, no… but, Daphne was for a while, weren't you, my love?'

Reggie thinking…

Jesus Christ!

This was going to be perfect.

The five of them sat around the dining table, ground floor, Stanley Crescent, drapes drawn, the lighting subdued with wall units picking out the elaborate molded plaster-work of the high ceiling – all lovingly restored under Reggie's supervision – Dire Straits, *Brothers In Arms*, on the sound system, no more than a whisper, despite what the Bang and Olufsen could deliver, and Eddy Wong busy in the kitchen... *the* Eddy Wong, of Wong's on Westbourne Park Road. Reggie had hired him in for the evening to organise the food, Eddy's boy's back and forth from the restaurant, Eddy, himself, taking care of last minute touches in Reggie's kitchen.

Said all he needed was a wok.

Cleaver.

High heat...

On demand.

Can't go far wrong with Chinese.

Indeed.

Reggie beaming, saying, 'I do hope everybody likes Peking duck.'

Daphne saying, 'Oh goodie, my favourite!'

And later...

Daphne loosening up on the ice-cold chardonnay, then the hot saki, telling them about her and Kenneth's trip to New York City earlier in the summer. Reggie wondering if they knew they weren't the first couple from west London had flown across the Atlantic – holding up her hand, laughing, saying, 'Talk to this,' the 'Talk' pronounced Talc as in 'Talcum Powder ... Daphne's idea of a Bronx accent.

Tucking into her toffee banana.

The last to finish.

Reggie finding her perversely attractive as she wiped her sticky mouth with the napkin, tried to refold the napkin, gave up, set it down beside her plate, Reggie leaning in close to her, saying – whispering, so nobody else could hear – 'What does Ken like, Daphne... does he like to tongue you out?'

Daphne not believing what she had heard.

Out of the blue like that.

Colouring.

Saying, this time everybody could hear, 'I do think some things are best left to the privacy of the bedroom, don't you?'

Darren, wishing he had caught what Reggie had said, thinking, 'Behind Closed Doors', why the fuck didn't The King ever record that? Not that Charlie Rich's version wasn't okay.

Reggie, off on one now, his favourite subject, saying, 'The holy trinity, the three T-s... essential for the mastery of exquisite sexual union. Timing... titillation... torture. When was it, last, you had exquisite sex, Daphne?'

Daphne unaware that none of this was for her benefit.

Reggie checking out her old man.

Seeing just how much shit he was willing to take.

Reggie saying, 'You can always tell a couple who are good together physically.... take Darren and Kiren, for example, don't the two of them positively glow.'

Darren thinking of the 'not moving first' game.

Kiren thinking the same.

Both smiling.

Reggie saying, 'Just look at them. Smug as two builders in a Transit.'

Kiren saying, 'What?'

Darren saying, 'You're losing the plot, Reggie.'

Reggie back with Daphne, off in an entirely different direction, saying, 'And now they've banned silicone tits from Page Three... hardly fair on all those tarts had the op, forked out all that good money.'

Knowing Daphne would have loved to have held up her hand, again, this time for real, say, 'Talk to the hand.'

No faux Bronx accent.

What was the other one?

'I'm all over it.'

Meaning, I've got it covered. It's under control.

Daphne finishing her toffee banana.

Looking to her husband for support.

Saying, 'I really don't have any opinion on Page Three girls, one way or the other.'

Ken saying, 'Never had to give it much thought, yourself, have you, love, nature having been more than benevolent in that department.'

Daphne saying, 'Kenneth!'

Kenneth.

Never, Ken.

Ken, well out of it, indulging fantasies that, any moment now, they would be throwing their car keys on the table, he could be off upstairs to one of the bedrooms, giving it to Kiren.

Hadn't taken his eyes off her all evening.

Reggie thinking, Who could blame him... state of his missus?

Ken saying, 'What do you mean, *Kenneth*? That dress, we're hardly talking trade secrets.'

Ken Lovatt...

Planing and Development Office, Hounslow Borough Council... Reggie treating him to a taste of the good life. Had Harry pick him and Daphne up from their place in Chiswick, give the neighbours a glimpse of the Bentley Turbo R. Before they sat down to eat, taking them up to the third floor, Reggie's private collection... Sandro Chia's Meditation, Poliakoff's Composition, Rouge, Noir, Blanc, Caro Maria Mariani's Sogno Profetico, two or three Rego's, all of them, Reggie telling them, showing off his preference for strong vibrant colour... Ken and Daphne following him around going 'Hmmm...' and 'Ah,' not knowing what the fuck to say about his paintings except Daphne, remarking, 'These must be worth an awful lot of money.'

Getting the point.

Fucking philistines.

Earlier, after Darren and Kiren had finally arrived, Reggie had introduced Darren as his associate, saying he took care of the 'wet' work. Ken had asked what it was, exactly, that wet work entailed, asking like he had no interest in hearing the answer, like he was making small talk at some business do, glass of white in one hand, cocktail sausage in the other...

Wondering just how soon before he could get away.

Darren had said to him, 'Let's hope you need never find out.'

Then: 'First hand, that is.'

Ken, now, saying, 'Anybody mind if I light up?'

Reggie offering him a cigar.

'Montecristo A, £28.50 a throw. Lew Grade, himself, smokes these.'

Ken, maybe not as drunk or stupid as everybody thought, saying, 'It's okay, Reggie. You've made your point.'

Taking a cigar, anyway.

Reggie saying, 'The way I see it, there's no point having money, you don't enjoy it, am I right, Darren?'

Darren was watching Daphne, smiling.

Reggie thinking, Christ! He's noticed it, too. The the way the daft bitch had started looking at him.

Like she was down the Palais De Dance.

On the pull.

Darren saying, 'Looks like you scored, Reggie.'

Reggie rolling his eyes to the ceiling.

Sad cow.

Actually thought he was interested.

16

'Darren, you're a shit, you know that, don't you?'
Alison on the telephone, nine-thirty the morning after Reggie Crystal's dinner party. Darren thinking, why the fuck had he ever given her Kiren's number.

In case of emergencies?

What the fuck could ever be that urgent?

Kiren stirring beside him.

Hand resting between his legs.

Cupping his balls.

Darren saying, 'Alison, God's truth… I had no idea they would move so fast.'

'Well, you're out of an office, let me tell you that.'

'Fucking stroll-on.'

'Never mind "fucking stroll-on," what about my wages?'

'Alison…'

'Two weeks, you owe me.'

'And you shall get it. What do you take me for?'

Kiren snuggling up to his back, pushing her pelvis against him. Alison saying, 'Darren, you forget, I've seen you operating.'

'You'll get it, all right.'

'Well just so we're clear on that point… there's always Ms. Shanks at the VAT Office, I'm sure she'd like to know where to find you.'

Fucking bitch.

Were all women the same?

Kiren, half awake now, stroking his prick from behind, still moving against him.

'Alison?'

The line going dead.

Darren taking Kiren's hand off his prick, moving away from her. Kiren, opening her eyes, saying, 'That's a first in our relationship, you know that?'

'What is?'

'You refusing me.'

Darren saying, again…

'Fucking stroll-on.'

Part Three
Half a Result...

Old George sat on an upright kitchen chair in his allotment shed, Plot 32, The Old Burial Site, with an army service revolver on his lap. The kitchen chair was tubular steel, cream painted, fablon covered seat and backrest, rescued from a skip... Old George couldn't remember how long ago. The army service revolver, he had taken from a decapitated army infantry captain in an apple orchard four miles from Sword Beach in Normandy, on June the Ninth, 1944. The army service revolver had been loaded when he'd found it.

Still was.

Same six .38 calibre bullets...

Had lain in the bottom drawer of his bedroom dresser, beneath a pile of his best shirts, ironed and neatly folded, since his discharge from the army in '47... every time the police announced an amnesty on fire-arms, his wife, Amie, saying, 'Go on, George, why don't you hand it in... ugly thing. You know I hate having it in the house.'

But George never had.

The gun brought back too many memories.

Not of the war...

The army infantry captain, head taken off his shoulders by a German eighty-millimetre shell, frayed blood vessels and muscle, top of his spine sticking out of the meat like a stick of sea-side rock with the colour sucked out – he had seen a lot worse than that by the time he got to Berlin...

But, of when he was young.

Of a time when he wouldn't have needed any loaded army service revolver to see off a bunch of young hooligans, coming down the allotments, three nights, already, this month, trampling everything under-foot...

The growing season in full swing, and nothing to show for it.

Old George uncomfortable on the upright chair, but still feeling himself start to nod off... remembering the Chinese couple, ran a restaurant, caught red-handed loading everybody's onions into sacks, hauling them into the back of their Escort van... fined fifty quid when it came up before the magistrate, it was in the local papers. The old dear with the bike, basket on the front, going round nicking all the strawberries. Kids from the council estate down the road, their mothers saying, 'Go over and get me a nice cabbage for your dinner, would you?'

But, this was different.

Vandalism for the sake of it.

Old George had worked Plot 32, The Old Burial Site, for 46 years, since 1949, two years after his discharge from the Army, saved him from a lifetime of up and down to the shops with Amie, once he retired from Wilkinson Sword.

Took first prize at the annual horticultural show every year with his onions, Showmaster, he swore by them... grew brassicas, spuds, leeks, carrots, marrow, none of those new-fangled vegetables all the Johnny-come-latelies were planting out, foreign stuff like garlic and peppers. Made Old George laugh, them coming down here full of their big ideas, lasting out one, maybe two seasons, once they found out how much work was involved. Their plots knee-deep in weeds till the next new lot arrived. Saying to them, when they asked his advice in the horticultural shop on Sunday morning, them in their waterproof coats and green wellies, 'You can t grow two things on the same patch of earth.'

Or: 'Digging... little and often, is what I always say.'

Thinking, now, It had to be the kids doing it. Who else, but kids?

Special extra-ordinary meeting of the local Horticultural Society.

Police called in...

What did they care?

Old George deciding, after the meeting, nothing else for it, he'd have to sort the little buggers out for himself.

Looking at his watch, shielding the glow of the torch from the shed window... 2 a.m., only ten minutes since he last checked the time.

The army service revolver on his lap, thinking of Veronique, in Rouen. What she did to him in her little room above the bakery. Amie had never done that for him... before or since.

And the two lads from engineers, went blind after drinking wood alcohol...

Shipped back to Blighty.

Bloody frogs.

Couldn't trust any of them.

Except Veronique.

Lovely lass.

The smell of fresh baked bread always reminding him of her.

What she did.

Old George glad he was past having to worry his head about that kind of nonsense any more...

Nodding off.

17

The thing about these days, having pubs with clear glass in the windows so you could see out, was Kevin was always interrupting whatever is was they were talking about with comments like, 'Get a look at the pair on that one... sweet fucking mother of Jesus, is that jail-bait or what?'

This, after they refurbished the Mason's Arms two years back. Nothing drastic, thank fucking Christ... took out the old carpet, varnished up the floor-boards, Music Hall posters framed and stuck up on the walls, called the back bar – used to be the public bar – the eating area, this for the office workers came in of a lunch-time.

Four in the afternoon.

All the office workers back at their terminals.

Or, in the company car park having a fag.

School's out...

Twyeford...

The reason Kevin was talking jail-bait.

One-track mind, Kevin.

Stoney saying, 'Will you just listen for once in your fucking life?'

Happy to be off on one.

Kevin had been talking about a Toyota Corrolla he was delivering back to a customer, parked up outside the main post office in Chiswick High Road, just five minutes, came out, there was the tow truck.

This being yesterday morning.

Before Dennis decided they should all get together, discuss Darren's proposition.

Kevin going through the usual… 'Have a heart, I was only inside for two minutes.'

Two minutes.

Five minutes.

What the fuck difference did it make?

The young geezer operating the winch saying, 'Sorry, mate, once the docket gets made out, nothing we can do about it.'

His partner, big geezer, mid-thirties, in the cab, taking in Kevin in his wing mirror, ready to climb out of the cab if his mate looked like he needed any assistance. Kevin, nothing to lose either way – he would bill the parking ticket to the customer – saying, 'Well, fuck you, too.'

Toyota Corrolla moving steadily up the ramp.

The young bloke, with the toggle control, saying, 'No call for that. I'm only doing my job.'

Kevin, finishing his story, saying, 'If I had a fiver for every cunt said that to me.'

Which was when Stoney began to wax philosophical, saying, 'What I don't get is this… these people, they say it like it's some excuse. Like, if they're only doing their job, it means they're only doing it for the money, right? Not cause they actually deep down and truly want to do it. In my book, that makes it even worse… doing it for the money.'

Dennis saying, 'Do you come out with some bollocks, or what?'

Which was when the two schoolgirls from Twyeford waltzed past, putting it out, looking in through the pub window, giggling when they saw Kevin.

Then, Kevin coming out with his jail-bait comment.

Dennis starting to lose it.

Meant to be on a pick-up for the shop, Transit parked out front on a double-yellow, picturing Eric's face, he told him the Transit got towed away, him inside, in the pub, listening to Kevin going on about how *he* got towed away…

You would have to have a sense of humour.

Saying, 'For fuck's sake, what do you think? Are we up for this, or what?'

Kevin saying, 'Bit of extra never did go amiss.'

Stoney, pissed off, saying, 'You two never listen to a fucking word I'm saying, do you?'

Dennis saying, 'No wonder Grace kicked you out.'

Kevin saying, 'Which reminds me, I'll have a word with Michelle, later.'

Dennis: 'And the rest.'

Kevin grinning.

Stoney saying to Dennis, 'What's that supposed to mean?'

Kevin saying, 'See if we can get you fixed up.'

'And the rest?'

'No, before that.'

Dennis saying, 'You mean about you always talking a load of old bollocks?'

'That's it.'

'Why Grace kicked you out?'

'Right.'

'Well, what about it, Stoney?'

Stoney saying, 'You just watch what you come out with, that's all, Dennis.'

Dennis thinking, Jesus fucking Christ!

Now, even, Stoney Todd thinking he could take a pop and get away with it.

18

Duncan and Carol sitting on the grass, Richmond Green, eating their lunch.

Duncan, hot salt beef on whole wheat, plenty of mustard.

'Make sure it's English.'

Carol, mozzarella, sun-dried tomato and fresh basil on ciabatta.

Saying, to the Italian woman in the sandwich bar, 'Lots of black pepper and a sprinkle of olive oil, please.'

Duncan looking at Carol's legs, bare from the knee, shoes off, feet tucked up beneath her backside, warm curve of her hips... thinking about Lindsay. How he liked to imagine her having an affair with another man, just to invest her with some sense of sexuality, convert her into a sexual creature. Pictured her up against a wall, somewhere dark and seedy, some Lotharian pumping into her, Lindsay screaming and biting, one bare leg bent, foot jammed into his backside.

Then, imagining doing that with Carol.

Wondering if their heights were compatible.

Whether height mattered.

Not knowing...

Having never fucked standing up, not once, in his whole life.

The other image:

Lindsay with a man's cock in her mouth.

His favourite.

Ludicrous.

Surrealistic.

Lindsay saying, the first time she saw his naked erection, 'Good God! And some women envy that?'

On the odd occasion when he and Lindsay still made love… usually in the morning, the two of them half-asleep, caught unawares before the steel barrier of mutual inhibition slid back into place between them.

Lindsay saying, after one-such occasion, 'You make love like it's a variation on needing a pee.'

Duncan asking, 'What does that mean?'

'Just one more physical chore needs to be done.'

Duncan saying, 'Well, thank you very much.'

Wishing he could discuss it with Carol, the two of them sitting here on the grass, everybody out taking advantage of a sudden hot spell after all the rain. How would she react if he told her that he and Lindsay had never made love anywhere apart from in a bed? Would she laugh? Would she feel sorry for him. Comfort him? Take pity…

Transport him to another world.

Where women enjoyed it…

As much as men.

Wanting to tell her that he had never been able to decide whether Lindsay was just not interested in sex, or just not interested in sex with him. How she never alluded to sex, gave him the come-on, subtlety or otherwise, never dressed to attract, never, ever, initiated sex, even on those drowsy half-awake mornings before the alarm went off…

Sometimes too late to warn them.

Then, taking breakfast together.

The both of them ashamed.

Feeling soiled.

Taking an extra five minutes in the shower.

Saying, now, to Carol, 'You should have something covering your neck.'

Slender.

White.

Impossibly long.

The length accentuated by the short cut of her hair.

Adding, 'This global warming business, I'm sure there's something they're not telling us, you know.'

Carol laughing, saying, 'What's this? Another conspiracy theory? I bet you were a right anorak when you were younger.'

A final piece of sun-dried tomato, rescued from the side of her sandwich, popped into her mouth.

Duncan saying, 'Not so much of the "When you were younger".'

Laughing.

Disguising his anger.

Carol sipping from her styrofoam cup, hers with the cross to denote sugar, saying, 'I always feel so silly asking for this... chocaccino. But, I do love it.'

'It's just what you're used to... cappuccino sounds every bit as stupid, when you think about it.'

Thinking of Lindsay.

Trying to remember the last time he had seen her naked.

Picturing Carol naked.

Carol saying, 'What do you think Jeff meant?'

'What?'

'As we were leaving... just now.'

Jeff Youdell, the news editor, as they were going down the stairs, head over the banister rail, looking down, saying, 'Careful, Carol, it's the quiet ones you have to watch out for...'

Laughing.

His head disappearing.

Duncan saying, 'I have absolutely no idea.'

Envying Carol her cigarette.

Marlboro Light.

Exaggerated exhalation of smoke.

Lips pouting.

Duncan wondering what her expression would be like in orgasm.

Lindsay saying, 'I don't like it when you look at me like that.'

Eyes closed.

Darkness.

19

Darren, on his mobile, watching the woman coming out the front door of number 32, the au pair on the phone, saying, 'No, I am sorry, she is in Paris.'

Darren saying, 'How long for?'

The au pair, some kind of Scandinavian la-di-da-di accent, probably Swedish, saying, 'I do not know this.'

The woman, Mrs Reece-Morgan, bold as brass, you had to hand it to her, seeing Darren on the pavement by the front gate, searching her bag for the car keys, lips pursed, how dreadfully inconvenient life could be, saying, 'I know, I know... I will get the cheque to you just as soon as I've sorted it out with my husband.' Then, 'In the meantime, I would very much appreciate it if you would stop chasing me from pillar to post.'

The au pair, inside the house, Darren could see her through the living room bay window, about eighteen, blonde, nice tits, still on the mobile saying, 'Hello, hello?' Darren, thinking, what a nice job Stoney had made of the windows, cancelling send, tucking the phone into his jacket, saying, 'I was in the neighbourhood, thought I'd try my luck.'

The woman stopping her side of the gate, sighing, saying, 'What are we talking about here? Nine hundred pounds or thereabouts? Is all this *really* necessary?'

Mrs Reece-Morgan.

Yes, he had to hand it to her.

Standing there in her beige and tan suit.

Expensively bobbed hair.

Saying, now, 'Hardly an amount for it to be worth your stalking me, surely?'

The job completed three weeks, now, Stoney already whingeing on about his money...

First it was: 'I'll need to give you a company cheque and the cheque book is at the office.' This, after her saying on the phone, Darren chasing her, 'What *was* the balance?' Darren telling her, staying patient, as if she didn't know the figure, 'Nine-hundred-and-eighty-two,' her saying, 'Can we do something with that?'

What they always said.

As if the world owed them something for nothing.

Darren saying, 'Mrs Reece-Morgan, we've already been through this.'

Her telling him the cheque would be in the post.

Big sigh...

Such a fuss over such a trivial matter.

Letting Darren know just how unreasonable he was being.

Bailiff's hovering, suppliers issuing writs, Alison on the blower telling him they were about to lose the office... and what about her wages?

Never rains but it pours.

Darren waiting four days, getting Alison to check the post first thing every morning, waiting for her to get back to him, tell him the eagle had landed, knowing the woman was a fucking liar... Mrs Reece-Morgan adamant that she had posted the cheque, saying, 'I do find it rather irritating that you should be doubting my word.'

Now, bang to rights, coming down the garden path, her au pair inside on the blower, saying, 'No, I'm sorry, she is in Paris.'

Fucking stroll-on.

Her *still* trying to brazen it out.

Darren saying, 'Off to catch your flight?'

No more pretence.

No more customer/supplier bullshit.

'I really don't see how my activities are any of your business.'

Darren saying, 'My side of the street, you owe somebody, your whole life is their business.'

Mrs Reece-Morgan not getting it.

Unaware that the rules had changed.

Saying, 'I believe I should warn you, your attitude is hardly likely to achieve the result you require.'

Opening the gate.

Walking round him.

Bottle-green Cherokee Jeep parked at the curb.

The kind of motor people who had trouble signing cheques always drove.

Darren coming between her and the driver's door.

Out on the street, now.

Mrs Reece-Morgan saying, 'Excuse me, do you mind?'

Postman, pushing his trolley on the opposite pavement, showing some interest, shuffling letters, moving on.

Darren saying, 'I don't see we have a problem, here. Just let me have a cheque, I'll be on my way.'

Mrs Reece-Morgan saying, 'I *beg* your pardon?' Then: 'Will you *please* step out of my way?' Then: 'You do realise, demanding money with menaces is a criminal offence?'

Darren realising the money was out the window, thinking, What the fuck... slapping the woman, open palmed across her face, her head snapping back, her going, 'Oh!' – more shocked than hurt.

Then surprising him.

Spitting in his face.

Screaming, 'Scum!'

Darren stepping in close, jabbing her hard in the stomach, her breath leaving her body, surprising him again as two false teeth on a gum plate flew over his right shoulder, Darren saying, 'This is your doing, you know that, don't you, you stupid bitch.'

Mrs Reece-Morgan on the ground, doubled over, hands to her stomach, crying.

Darren saying, 'Get up, for fuck's sake.'

Trying to take her arm.

Mrs Reece-Morgan pulling away.

The postman running across the road.

Young bloke, early twenties...

Going bald, already.

'What the fuck's going on?'

Darren, not sure why he had punched the woman.

Punched her so hard.

Mrs Reece-Morgan vomiting, now.

Darren turning to the kid, all he needed, Postman Pat on a mercy mission, saying, 'And you can fuck off if you know what's good for you.'

20

Darren, from the bed, saying to Kiren, 'You know, there is this hotel in Memphis, the Peabody Hotel, right across the road from Graceland, has these ducks that step out of the elevator at eleven o'clock every morning, spend the day in the hotel lobby fountain... the tourists love them. Guide books call them the legendary Peabody Hotel ducks.'

Kiren just showered.

Smelling of...

Kiehl?

Geurlain Issima?

Kept it all in her bathroom cabinet, the Guerlain Issima in squat blue jars, gold covers, looked expensive, was expensive. The Kiehl in plastic containers, the modest packaging fooling nobody.

Kiren not sure if it was a Geurlain Midnight Secret morning... then deciding on the Orchid Oil.

Body Shop.

Wrapped in a cream bath towel, trailing wet footprints across the bedroom carpet, saying, 'Have you ever been to Memphis?'

Knowing how much he loved The King.

Saying to Darren, one time, 'Put it this way... a ball of lard like that came on to me, no matter how rich, I would just *not* be interested.'

Then: 'Uggh!'

Teasing.

Darren saying, 'But, the voice, Kiren, you have to listen to the voice.'

Then: 'What about Pavarotti? Does anybody care that he's a sad fat bastard.'

Kiren, saying, 'Yeah, well, I wouldn't let Luciano fuck me, either.'

Losing Darren with the first name.

Darren, now, watching Kiren drop the bath towel, climb into her knickers, La Perla's, that's what she called them, saying, 'I read about it... the ducks, I mean.'

La Perla's?

Knickers?

Made no sense to Darren.

Kiren saying, 'Tell me, Darren, did you ever leave the country, yet?'

Darren ignoring that.

Thinking about the woman on her hands and knees in the road, vomiting.

Wondering if that was how The King had looked.

The bathroom at Graceland.

His final moments...

Throwing up blood.

Kiren saying, earlier, before her shower, 'I just don't believe how some people let themselves go, there's no excuse for it, really, you don't have to be well off or anything.'

Talking about the Milky.

Darren's description.

Coming across the road when he hit the woman.

Pigeon toes.

Waddling like a duck.

Kiren saying, 'If you have pigeon toes, how can you waddle like a duck?'

Which was how Darren got on to the Peabody Hotel...

The legendary ducks.

Graceland.

Kiren, dressed now, white T-shirt, black designer jeans, no bra, feet still bare, saying to Darren, still in bed, not looking like he was going anywhere, 'You can stay here, Darren, but you don't live here.'

Finding her shoes.

Black with gold trim.

Chanel, Old Bond Street.
Then: 'You ever hit me, that's it, you know that, don't you?'
Darren trying to remember how long it had taken the scorch marks to disappear.
Kiren's neck.
Thinking:
Women.
Who the fuck could understand them?

21

The two of them at an outside table, Palatino's, Moscow Road, just up from the Greek Church, Queensway, Reggie saying to Darren, 'You see, Darren, your problem is this... you're sat here thinking, What I wouldn't give for a decent fry-up instead of this shit. Limited horizons, do you see what I'm saying?'

Still early.

Everybody rushing to work.

Sad bastards...

Reggie saying, 'We're all European now, Darren.'

Darren staring at the plate of pastries... croissant, brioche... the two of them drinking cappuccino, thinking, Fucking mind-reader, or what? Picturing the plate, too hot to touch, eggs, crispy bacon rashers – streaky, lots of fat – tomatoes, mushroom, fried bread, bubble to mop up the egg yoke, mug of tea...

Where was the problem in that?

Then thinking: Fuck being European.

Watching Reggie dunk his croissant, coffee dripping on to the blue-check tablecloth as he leaned forward, brought the croissant to his open mouth, all the while staring at Darren.

Saying, 'You want to hang on to a girl like Kiren, she's got style... breeding.'

Reggie saying this...

Dropping damp croissant all over the table.

'Meaning?'

Reggie, shrugging his shoulders, saying, 'I'm sure it's none of my business.'

Darren saying, 'Too fucking right.'

Then: 'It's a bit early in the day, Reggie.'

Reggie saying, 'You have to remember, Darren, I'm on your side.'

Darren, not sure if he liked the idea.

Reggie Crystal being on his side.

Thinking: Fucking pervert.

Reggie changing the subject. Darren, missing the first part, hearing Reggie say, 'Did you see it?', saying, 'Come again?'

Reggie saying, 'Last night's *Standard*.'

'What about last night's *Standard*?'

Reggie quoting, 'Gangs cash in on £500 million London home fraud.' Saying, 'Crooked landlords raking in as much as £10,000 a week,' laughing, adding, 'And the. rest, eh, Darren?'

Darren saying, 'What would I know?'

'Exactly.'

'Benefit going direct into the landlord's pocket. What could be sweeter?'

'Is there a point to all this?'

'One billion lost annually to the public purse due to fraud, would you credit that?'

Then: 'The point being this, Darren... any problem, I like to think I'd be the first to know about it.'

'You're losing me, Reggie.'

Darren watching the three teenage girls coming towards them along the pavement, just finished their hotel breakfast, out early taking in the sights, Darren knowing they were Yanks before they even opened their mouths... the girls stepping off the pavement, avoiding the dosser, still asleep two doorways up. All of them overweight, kitted out in baggy T-shirts, baggy shorts, blue baseball hats, Darren thinking, Everybody going on about The King, how much excess he put on towards the end, but, that was nothing to the state of some of them. The girls talking to a motorcycle dispatch rider parked at the curb, checking an *A-Z* he kept in the webbing on his petrol tank. One of them saying, 'The Royal Gardens of Kensington, are we close?' The dispatch rider, not bothering to look up, pointing towards Queensway. Another of the girls saying, 'We thank you kindly.'

Kawasaki 550.

What the kid was riding.

The girls looking in through the window of Palatino's, passing Reggie and Darren's table, Reggie saying, 'Keep you warm in winter, eh, Darren?'

'Do me a favour.'

'All you have to do is ask.'

One of the girls looking back.

Darren staring straight through her, saying to Reggie, 'The problem with people offering you favours, this big red warning light always comes on in my head.'

'As well it should, Darren. Nothing is for nothing, am I right?'

Finished with the croissant.

Wiping his fingers one by one, then his mouth, with a paper napkin, smiling at Darren. The motorcycle dispatch rider's short-wave bursting into life, static and garbled instruction from his controller. Reggie saying, 'Noisy bastard,' the rider stowing his *A-Z*, starting the Kawasaki, taking off along Moscow Road towards Notting Hill Gate, one boot trailing the ground.

Darren saying, 'They're all fucking cowboys.'

Reggie saying, 'How it works, Darren, is this... you buy a property, terraced house, nice on-the-up middle class neighbourhood, pay the going rate. You convert to flats, let it out to Rastas, punk rockers, students, Bangladeshis just in off a British Airways' undercarriage... all of a sudden the local residents are worried their property values will nose-dive. They're looking back nostalgically to the halcyon days when their only concern was whether they should support the introduction of CPZs... are you with me on this?'

Darren saying, 'Don't patronise me, Reggie.'

Then: 'This coffee is stone fucking cold.'

Reggie not offering to order a refill, saying, 'You start buying into the area, shave three grand here, five grand there, nothing spectacular, but it all adds up.'

Sophia came out to clear their table. She and her old man, Michael, owned Palatino's, had wanted to pass the business on to their only son, George, only he decided he wanted to be a urology consultant instead.'Kids, eh,' Reggie had said, when

Sophia told him, 'They don't know when to be grateful.' Sophia, leaning over the table, could smell the sweat, saying to Reggie, now, 'You want more coffee?' Reggie shaking his head. After she had gone back inside, they could see her through the plate-glass window, totalling up their bill from a chit she kept on a spike next to the till. Reggie saying to Darren, 'Only place in London you don't get a free refill… you have to hand it to her.'

Then: 'So, Darren, what happens next?'

'You're enjoying this, Reggie, don't let me spoil it for you.'

'No, tell me.'

'You reconvert the first place you bought?'

'After removing the undesirables. Property values go back up… meanwhile, you're renting out for eight hundred a week on the other properties, paying four hundred a month in mortgage. Company lets… Americans, Japanese businessmen, they're always favourite. Once you can afford to buy outright…'

'Piece of piss.'

'You know what they say, Darren. You want to make money, don't waste your time working. You'll be too busy working to find the time to make any money.'

Then: 'It's important everybody knows their rightful place within an organisation. There have been problems of late. An unwanted focusing of attention.'

Darren spreading his hands, saying, 'Any way I can help, Reggie, any way at all.'

'A safe pair of hands, I'm sure.' Then, Reggie saying, 'House clearance is how I see you.'

Darren saying, 'House clearance?'

Reggie looking at his watch, saying, 'Lovely girl, Kiren, you must bring her over more often.'

Darren saying, 'Don't even think about it.'

Reggie saying, 'I wouldn't be human.'

Sophia hovering with the bill, Reggie motioning towards Darren, saying, 'High maintenance woman, am I right?'

Sophia placing the saucer with the bill in front of Darren, Darren checking the damage, thinking, For fuck's sake, saying, 'I'd have you, you know that, don't you?'

Reggie saying, 'Chance would be a fine thing.'
Darren paying Sophia.
Feeling sick.
Not sure if it was the brioche.

22

Darren digging a hole for himself.
Calling Stoney 'mate'.
Then jumping in.

After Stoney said, 'Where's the catch?', Darren saying, 'Trust me.'

The two of them in what used to be The Builder's Arms, Young's pub, top of King Street, near the Broadway. now done up, called The Hungry Hop, what the fuck did Darren care? Handing Stoney the key to the Banham Street flat, saying, 'As long as you like, mate, till you get fixed up.' One of Reggie's places. Stoney nursing a pint of Carlsberg Extra, sat there in the green combat vest and grey track-suit bottom he always wore, Darren saying, 'The old girl downstairs, she's deaf as a coot, you can make as much racket as you like.'

'Just till I get sorted with Grace.'
'Ask me, you're better off without her.'
'I didn't ask you.'
'All right, whatever.'
'And say again about the rent.'
Not believing.
Not trusting.
Too good to be true.
'You let me worry about that, okay?'

Stoney, looking at Darren, saying, 'My old man used to tell me, Never trust a bloke who calls you mate, especially if he sticks a *trust me* in front of it.'

'Your old man always right, was he?'
'Far as I know.'

Darren realising his mistake...
Too late.
Stoney off on one.
The complete history of Fulham... his old man, Arthur Todd, one of the firm, a cleaner.
'Cleaner?'
'What they used to call anybody took care of the dirty work.
...Gambling man, spent half his life down the dog track, used to be big business in those days, White City, Park Royal, Crayford, Stamford Bridge, the 'Big Field' at Dagenham... his old man thick as thieves with the Gadds, ran all the barrows down the North End Road, knocked around with Johnny Bindon, his old man saying how Johnny Bindon used to boast he had the biggest prick in Fulham, only, if the truth be told, he *was* the biggest prick in Fulham, always shooting his mouth off, some bird or other in tow, it was only a question of time, that geezer doing him with the baseball bat down the Crooked Billet...
Way off his patch.
Walthamstow.
Darren saying, 'Johnny Bindon? Didn't he end up poured into one of the concrete pylons when they were building Hammersmith Flyover?'
'That was Ginger Powell.'
'Silly me.'
Stoney, not finished yet.
Not by a long chalk.
Saying: 'Saw him, one time, put this geezer down. Not a big bloke, my old man, this geezer must have weighed in twice his size. Outside the Swan, in Fulham Broadway... one Sunday lunch-time. Our mum had sent me down there to tell him his dinner was on the table. This geezer comes up from behind, my old man must have had eyes in the back of his head, one jab with his elbow, this geezer is stretched out on the pavement. My old man looks at me, says, "Well, you don't argue with a big man, now, do you, son?"'
Darren saying, 'I envy you, you know that, Stoney.'
Stoney, surprised.
'You? Envy me?'

'Having an old man you could look up to.'

Thinking of his own old man.

Worthless piece of shit.

Stoney saying, 'You know what he did, one time, my old man? I had three kids chasing me. I'm on the front door step banging away, hoping my old man will get to the door and open it before they reach me. The old man opens the door, sees what's going on, slams it shut in my face.'

'What happened then?'

'What do you think happened then? What happened then is these three kids beat the shit out of me. After they've gone my old man lets me in, the old lady screaming blue murder at him. My old man tells me, "Son, you have to learn to fight your battles in this world."'

Then: 'Still going strong, he is… despite spending more time than is healthy down The Charing Cross Hospital.'

'It's always the short ones, right?'

'And the rest.'

'Too fucking right, mate.'

That word, again.

Mate.

Stoney saying, 'It won't be for long, this arrangement. Me and Grace, we'll be back together again before you know it.'

'Let's hope so, Stoney, for your sake.'

'Minor hiccup, is all.'

'In the meantime…'

Darren sliding the list of names across the table, the three names Reggie had given him: 'Anybody asks, these are the geezers you will be sharing with.'

Stoney not getting it, saying, 'I thought you told me I had the place to myself?'

'And so you do, Stoney. This is for if anybody comes round snooping… you just tell them these are the blokes you are sharing with, right?'

Stoney still not getting it.

Darren thinking, Jesus Christ! Ignorant as shit, some people.

Deciding not to bring up the business of the old lady downstairs.

Leave that till Stoney got settled in.

23

Alison wasn't sure yet whether she hated Reggie Crystal or whether she merely loathed him... or, even, which was the stronger emotion.

Either way, she couldn't deny he fascinated her.

Like a clammy warm-blooded reptile.

Most of all...

It was his shoes.

Brass buckles?

Two hours into her first morning with Sterling Realty – demure olive-green shop front, name picked out in small gold lettering on the glass window, frontage in Holland Park Avenue under the shadow of the poplars – Alison had decided that Reggie Crystal was a weirdo. By mid-afternoon of that first day she had concluded that he was a sicko-weirdo.

Not sure if she should be grateful to Darren.

Or hate him forever.

Darren, on the phone, saying, 'You'll like him, I know you will... just give him time. And he's a better payer than I ever was.'

'That doesn't mean a lot, Darren.'

'Alison! Haven't I always seen you all right?'

'You still owe me for two weeks. There isn't some kind of finder's fee.'

'I know that, Alison. You'll get your money.'

Alison showing up on the first morning, ten o'clock sharp. Expecting a staff of three or four people, just Reggie at the front desk sorting through the mail, saying, 'Bills, bills, and more bills.'

Then: 'You must be Alison... this will be your desk. I'm through the back there. Your job, as far as is humanly possible, will be to prevent any persons from proceeding past your desk and through to my desk.... it's that simple.'
Then: 'De Souza?'
Alison's surname.
Alison Katherine de Souza.
Used to the lads, when they asked her, saying, 'De Souza? What a weird name. Is it Portuguese?'
Or Spanish.
Alison telling them, 'No, it's Irish.'
'But, you don't sound Irish.'
'Maybe, that's because I come from Northolt.'
Incredibly boring.
All Reggie Crystal said was, 'Are you familiar with the work of your namesake... wrote marches... very stirring *oeuvre*.'
Introducing her to the terminal.
Lists of properties.
Rental values.
Current occupancies.
A morning spent surfing the information.
Familiarising.
Not one person coming in through the door from the street. Just before lunch, Alison saying, 'How come?'
Reggie saying, 'My dear girl, we mustn't try to run before we can walk.'
Alison saying, 'This is a letting agency?'
Reggie grinning.
Alison, not in control, obliged to fill the silence, saying, 'Your clients contract you to manage their properties, arrange suitable tenants, collect rents, take care of any building maintenance, isn't that how it goes?'
Darren, over the phone, later, when she told him what she had said, saying, 'You said that to Reggie? You daft cow, he owns those properties, all of them.'
All Alison could say was, 'All of them?'
Feeling exactly what Darren had called her...
A daft cow.
Reggie still grinning, saying, 'This is your first day, you can't

expect to be *au fait* with everything on your first day.'

Then: 'You'll find a set of keys in that top right hand drawer. If I'm not around, just lock up when you go out for lunch… there's a nice little Italian, Fredo's, down on the right. They do a set lunch for six-fifty.'

Alison saying, 'You think I can afford six pounds-fifty a day for lunch?'

'Yes, well, that would depend on your priorities. The pub on the corner of Lansdown Road does a perfectly reasonable Shepherd's Pie, so I'm told.'

Not what he said.

More, *how* he said it.

Alison thinking, Supercilious bastard! Saying, 'I'll just grab a sandwich most days, and a drink.'

Already wondering how long she would be able to take it.

Just him and her.

Day in, day out.

No light relief.

Saying to Darren, when he rang her two nights later, see how she was getting on, 'The job is fine, the money is fine… it's just him. He spooks me off, gives me the creeps. You know some people, there's a physical reaction, they touch you and you come out in goose-pimples? I'm not sure I know how to explain it. Is he gay, or something?'

Darren laughing.

Saying, 'You're expecting Reggie Crystal to come on to you, you'd better forget it.'

'I didn't say that.'

'You've worked there three days, the poor bastard hasn't tried to get inside your knickers, that makes him an old queen, am I right?'

'That's not what I meant.'

'As it happens, you were closest with the "or something".'

'Surprise me.'

'He likes to hang himself from ceilings.'

'You're joking!'

'I kid you not.'

'I don't think I'll ever be able to look him in the eye again, you've told me that.'

Then, laughing, 'Does he wear a tutu?'
'How the fuck would I know?'
Then: 'Well, at least, he's harmless.'
Darren not wanting to agree or disagree.
Deciding…
That was another story.

24

Stoney's voice on the mobile... the mobile, One to One, under Kiren's bed somewhere, Kiren gone, Darren having to search both sides before he found it.

'...that woman we did the job for...'

Darren on one elbow, listening, staring at Kiren's Welsh dresser, unaware that it was a Welsh dresser, unaware that it was anything... his mind not yet in focus, his old man looming over him saying, 'In your dreams you can fuck who you want.'

Dressed for the office.

Sports jacket, check-shirt, tie, tan slacks...

Jesus Christ!

...black lace-up shoes.

Fucking state of him.

The kitchen table, Glenthorne Road.

Darren, sitting at the table, saying, 'I fuck who I want anyway, you sad git.'

Darren's mother saying, 'Eat your breakfast the both of you, before it gets cold.'

Hoping scrambled eggs and bacon would deflect the row.

Darren seeing his parents from a child's perspective, faces huge, filling his vision...

Coming awake.

Thinking: Is this what Alzheimer's is like?

Everything nonsense?

Stoney saying, 'It was the double-barrel rang a bell.'

Darren saying to Stoney, 'What the fuck do you mean, "Intensive care?"'

'West Middlesex Hospital... internal bleeding. Ruptured

spleen, they reckon in the paper. Happened right outside her own front door. The doctors say her condition is stable, but, critical, whatever that means.'

Darren hoping he was still dreaming, wanting to be back at the kitchen table in Glenthorne Road, one more fight with his old man, his old lady crying. Darren – then, as now – saying, 'This is all I fucking need.'

Stoney saying, 'You and me, both, pal.'

Wondering how Stoney had made the connection.

Stoney saying, 'Two witnesses saw the geezer. ... the milkman and an au pair.'

Now, awake.

Realising why Stoney was ringing.

Saying, 'Bit unfortunate, timing and all that.'

'What?'

'No, I didn't get it, yet.'

'You've lost me, Darren.'

'Your money... the cheque. She didn't pay me, yet.'

'Well, that's a piss-off.'

'Is that all you can think to say?'

Then: 'Poor woman could peg any minute.'

Taking the piss.

'It's all right for you... what about her old man, he'll cough, won't he?'

'I'm sure he will, Stoney, but it might show a little respect if we waited a while, don't you think?'

'How about you pay me up front? You can stand the difference till you get it.'

'That's as may be.'

'It's coming up to three weeks, Darren. Besides, I've got Grace's birthday to think about.'

'Still living in hope, are we? You're a daft twat, Stoney.'

'Is this a yes or a no?'

'I'll need to think about it.'

Darren breaking the connection, telescoping the aerial, dropping the phone on the floor... Stoney's cash-flow problems the last thing on his mind right now.

Seeing the woman on her knees in the road.

Breath knocked out of her.

Gasping.

Remembering telling Kiren, that evening, not knowing it was going to get serious. Few glasses of wine, some skunk Kiren got from the *Big Issue* vendor on the corner of the road by the new supermarket... Kiren getting off on the story, saying, 'I want to know everything, tell me what was going on in your mind the exact moment you hit her.'

Saying: 'Did it feel good?'

Then: 'As good as sex?'

Then, when Darren wouldn't answer, saying, 'Do you wish you hadn't done it... wish you could turn back the clock, make it so it never happened?'

Darren saying, 'The daft bitch had it coming.'

'Is that how you saw it?'

'I didn't see anything. I just lost it, that's all.'

Now thinking, If I only could...

Turn back the clock.

Intensive care.

Jesus fucking Christ.

Why me, God? Why me?

Kiren wrapping her arms round his neck, legs round his thighs, the two of them in the kitchen door, Darren having trouble keeping his balance, kettle boiling, Kiren saying, 'Do me now, Darren, here, like this.'

Only afterwards saying, 'You ever hit me...'

And the rest.

Darren, now, lying in her bed, not wanting to get up, face the day, wishing he had given her one, right there and then.

Teach the fucking bitch a lesson.

Who the fuck did she think she was?

Rolling out of bed, in the bathroom, pissing straight down the middle, could make all the noise he wanted with the flat to himself, Kiren off early to meet her old man off the train at Paddington, lunch at Harvey Nichols...

'On the Fifth.'

How Kiren put it.

Darren wondering if he was ever going to get the invite... Air-Vice Marshal James Arthur Fleming (retired), Windcroft, the family seat out near Winchester, best silverware on the

table, special bottle up from the cellar, the old man saying, 'I've been hearing so much about you... pleasure to meet up, at last.'
  Brandy.
  Cigars.
  Like fuck.
  In your dreams, Darren.
  In the shower, now, the water scalding, Darren's back smarting from where Kiren had gouged her nails through his flesh, Kiren saying, 'Don't let's get predictable, Darren.'
  Sadistic bitch.
  Dressing, then ringing Reggie at the office.
  Alison answering.
  'Sterling Realty, may I help you?'
  'It's me. Is Reggie around?'
  Alison, pretending she was funny, saying, 'Hold the line, I'll just ask him if he's in.'
  Darren, humming to himself while he waited...
  Maybe I didn't love you
  Quite as often as I could have...
  What kind of Queen's fucking English was that?
  Wondering why he had never got round to giving Alison one.
  Reggie coming on the line, saying, 'Darren, just the man.'
  'Reggie —'
  'Mrs Reece-Morgan, right?'
  Darren thinking, How the fuck?
  Reggie saying, 'I've just come off the blower. Her husband is anxious to have a word.'
  'I don't get this.'
  'Well, you wouldn't, would you.'
  Then: 'Relax... it's not like you think.'
  Darren thinking, Fuck me, what's going on?
  Saying: 'Fuck me.'
  Reggie saying, 'Careful, Darren. One fine day I might take you-up on that.'

25

Duncan saying about the young black woman moved into the house next door, the house divided into flats, her flat on the first floor next to Duncan and Lindsay's bedroom.

Standing beside Carol at her desk, terminus she shared with cinema reviews, restaurants and gardening, Carol saying, 'Black woman? I don't think you're supposed to say black woman.'

Duncan explaining to her how the ragga reggae started up at eleven o'clock every night, went on till six in the morning, everything shaking off the walls, the bass like an earthquake. The black woman, under twenty-five, totally anti-social, nocturnal peer group... Carol saying, 'Nocturnal peer group?'... round her place every night, saying things to Duncan like, 'You are a dead person,' or, 'One more complaint letter you are buried six feet deep.' Duncan, before he started calling the police – the only way to get them to come round, threaten to go next door commit a breach of the peace himself – confronting the woman, trying to reason with her, face to face interaction, getting back only hostility, saying to Carol there was a whole catalogue of psychological deficiencies going on in the woman's brain, that she was unable to grasp even the basics of human interpersonal skills. Then Duncan saying, 'Black woman? I'm not supposed to call her a black woman?'

'Not if it's used in a derogatory sense, you're not.'

'Carol, my nights are a living hell because she's got four-foot bass bins and is a borderline psychotic, not because she is a *black* woman.'

'So, why mention it at all?'
'I'm going to get a coffee… you want one?'
Machine out in the hall.
Top of the stairs.
'No, really?'
'I suppose I shouldn't have mentioned she was a woman, either?'
'Now you're getting there.'
'Or, that she was young… am I being ageist mentioning that she was young?'
'Duncan, you're being silly.'
Then: 'Why don't you take it up with the landlord?'
'It's a property company. They don't give a shit as long as the Benefit Office send them a rent cheque every week.'
'Poor Duncan.'
Duncan not sure if he was being teased.
Unhappy at the way Carol had said, 'You're being silly.'
Just the way Lindsay said it.

26

It was Rosy Reece, nineteen at the time, hairdresser's assistant, girl from the valley – 'valley' pronounced var-lee, the 'var' as in car, the 'lee' as in Marvin – who, two days before the wedding, had convinced Terry that they should re-invent themselves, introduce an upmarket feel to their name, impress those snotty London bastards when they made the move to the Big Smoke. Terry Morgan... Rugby League at Junior level, car mechanic with his old man's business, bit on the side buying motors at auction, selling them on, moved from motors, through caravan homes, to property, holiday lets up along the Gower Peninsula, slum terraces in Cardiff, made a tidy sum when they started redeveloping, his old man saying, 'Too good for us, already, our Terry is,' despite he could still drink the old bastard under the table any night of the week down the Social. Big hands, big shoulders, a nose he wasn't comfortable breathing through...

Legacy from the rugby days.

Not sure he could live with Terrance Reece-Morgan.

But, Rosy being Rosy.

Or, rather, Rosy being Rosemary.

She got her way.

That had been in 1976, twenty-one years ago, Terrance the only one still called her Rosy, and now she was on a respirator, the doctors not sure if she would live.

Fuck lot of good the double-barrel was to her, now.

Flying into Gatwick, Iberian Airways, cut short his stay at the villa in Malaga, too many tourists this time of the year, anyway, scouting the bars for Matts-Brink Robbers, all the decent tottie tied-up working the bars for a living. ... wondering what kind of fucking mess he was coming home to...

Rosy, dead?

No, that couldn't happen.

No matter who she'd taken to fucking around with.

Ordering a last scotch from the stewardess before she stowed the trolley, watching pink spray the tops of the clouds, thinking, Rosy from the Valley, how she had changed, become a woman he never knew, using his money to alienate herself from him, losing the accent, even. Pissed off with him that the one thing he would never do for her – the only thing – was to call her Rosemary. Rosy saying, 'You can take the boy out of the boyo, but you can't take the boyo out of the boy.'

Whatever the fuck that meant.

The stewardess clearing trays, collecting glasses, making sure seats were in an upright position.

That *ping* on the intercom.

Then, the Captain's voice, saying, 'We shall be commencing our final approach into Gatwick very shortly. Please extinguish all cigarettes and ensure that your seat-belts are securely fastened. Thank you for flying Iberian... we hope your flight has been a pleasant one.'

The 737 sinking rapidly.

Banking.

Terrance's stomach reaching up for his throat.

The cabin now silent – even the kids.

You could hear the flaps coming up, the pilot losing height, boosting the jets to compensate for the extra drag.

It would be dark when they got down.

If they ever did.

Terrance cursing Rosy.

Forcing him to fly standby.

Hands gripping the arm-rests, knuckles white, vowing that if he ever got out of this alive, screw Rosy and her big ideas...

Next time he walked on solid ground.

Call him Terry...

Why don't you?

27

Michelle saying, 'Very kinky!'
First time he had suggested it, back when they were still married. Kevin joking, saying to Michelle, 'We got two kids, already, how many more you want before you're twenty?'

Afterwards, Michelle complaining that it hurt.

Weeks later, Kevin forgotten it as a bad idea, Michelle saying, 'You know, if you want, I don't mind.'

Tight.

Very tight.

Michelle, all over. Anything to keep her man happy, that was Michelle. The two of them upstairs in Michelle's bedroom – used to be their bedroom – Michelle, one eye on the clock to pick the kids up from school. It was Kitty's birthday, six years old, already, Michelle was going to take her and her sister to the McDonald's, party upstairs with some of her class-mates. Kevin had bunged her twenty notes when he arrived, that and the Cindy Doll, Michelle holding the notes, two tens, saying, 'This for services about to be rendered, is it, Kev?' Kevin laughing, 'For the kid's do, you daft bitch. Day I have to pay for it, I'll be losing my touch.' Ashtray on the duvet between them, both smoking Kevin's Marlboro Lights, the phone ringing from miles away, Kevin saying about the duvet cover, orange with big white spots, the only new addition to the bedroom since Michelle had kicked him out, saying, 'Need fucking sun glasses, sleep in here.' Michelle, droll as ever, saying, 'That's not a problem ever going to concern you, is it, Kev?' Kevin saying, about the phone, still ringing in the hallway downstairs, 'You going to answer that, or what?'

Running his hand between her legs.

Michelle saying, 'Make it easy for a girl, why don't you?' Pushing his hand away, going down the stairs, eventually calling up to him, 'It's your brother.'

'Dennis?'

'How many brothers have you got?'

Kevin saying, 'Oh, fuck,' then, at the foot of the stairs, taking the phone from Michelle, her grinning, stroking his balls, hearing his brother say, 'I thought I might find you there.'

Kevin saying, 'So what?'

Michelle, behind him, now, her tongue in his ear. Kevin going stiff, Michelle reaching round, taking hold of him.

Kevin saying, 'Jesus.'

Dennis saying, 'It's just you ought to make up your fucking mind, that's what.'

Slow strokes.

To the hilt.

Dennis saying, 'It's not fair on Monica, it's not fair on Michelle.'

Kevin saying, 'Hark at big broth… is that why you rang, to give me a lecture?'

A low groan.

Couldn't help himself.

Dennis saying, 'This business with Darren, you up for it, or what?'

Michelle round the front now, on her knees on the hallway carpet, taking him in her mouth, Kevin saying, 'Oh, fuck!'

Dennis saying: 'What does that mean?'

Kevin saying, 'I don't need it, Dennis, I really don't.'

Then: 'What does Stoney think?'

'Says he's up for it as long as nobody gets hurt.'

Kevin saying, 'I don't know, Dennis. It doesn't feel right.'

Sharp intake of breath.

Michelle's tongue playing games.

Dennis saying, 'Half the fucking sheds are derelict, anyway, what's the fucking problem, torching a few empty sheds?'

'So, why should it be worth five hundred notes to Darren?'

Then 'Ah!'

Like an electric shock going through his body.
Michelle easing off, drawing him back from the brink.
Kevin saying, 'Don't stop.'
Dennis saying, 'What?'
Michelle taking Kevin deep into her mouth, cheeks puckering as she drew on him, continued to draw in him, Kevin, unable to take it, saying, 'Oh, Jesus Christ, fuck!'
Michelle swallowing.
Dennis, falling in, saying, 'You filthy bastard!'
Kevin saying, 'What?'
Dennis slamming down the phone.
Back upstairs, on the bed, the two of them still laughing, Kevin saying, 'Bit of a puritan, our Dennis,' wondering why he was still coming round so much, now he didn't need to tease Michelle on taking in Stoney as a lodger. Recognising Michelle's serious look, thinking, 'Oh, no… here we go.'
Remembering why he was happy to get away from Michelle in the first place.
Thought too much.
That was her trouble.
Michelle, surprising him, saying, 'The first time you ever fucked me, was it because I was black?'
Out of the blue.
Just like that.
Kevin thinking, Dodgy territory.
Saying: 'I fucked you because I fancied you, why else?'
Michelle saying, 'But, why did you fancy me? Did you fancy me because I was black?'
Kevin, not able to tell Michelle the truth… most blokes fucked birds as and when they could, it was as simple as that. Saying, 'We're talking a long time ago, here, Michelle.'
'You don't remember?'
'What? Why I fucked you?'
Thinking: Fucking mine-field.
Michelle saying, 'Most blokes I've been with, I know it was because I was black, they wanted to shag me.'
'Even the black geezers?'
Trying for laughs.
Some fucking hope.

Michelle saying, 'There haven't been any black geezers.'

Kevin saying, 'Really?' Then, up on his elbows, now, looking down at Michelle, saying, 'I don't see you have a problem, I really don't. If they weren't fucking you because you were black, they would be fucking you because you were a bird... that's the way blokes are, pure and simple.'

Michelle saying, 'What about fucking me because I'm me?'

Kevin saying, 'Don't be a daft bitch.'

Michelle saying, 'What about us, now, the second time round? Do you fuck me now, because I'm me, Michelle?'

Kevin saying, 'I don't need all this.'

Michelle saying, 'That's no fucking answer.'

Kevin saying, 'Michelle, you're an accommodating woman, and you have a nice little body, despite you've had two kids.'

Michelle saying, 'Kevin, you're a bastard.'

Then: 'Oh, fuck! I'm going to be late.'

The kids.

Kitty's birthday party.

Rolling off the bed.

Knickers.

Black 501's.

French Connection crop-top.

Rebok Classics, no socks, laces loose.

Saying to Kevin, still on the bed, not looking like he was in any hurry, '*Accommodating*? What does that mean, *accommodating*?

'Because I take it up the arse?'

Part Four:
No messin'…

*I*t was one of his bird scarers woke Old George. Sardine cans with the peeled back lid still attached, Heinz soup or baked bean tins, silver foil trays from the supermarket packaging – frozen puddings, microwave dinners – Old George hung them by pieces of string from bamboo canes so they rattled together the slightest gust of wind...

Or, if anybody knocked into them.

Most of the scarers up at the end by the young brassicas this time of year, spring cabbage, winter cauliflower, purple sprouting broccoli, wood-pigeons loved them, fat bastards.

Hearing it, now.

Could be the fox.

Two cans clattering together in the darkness. Way down the end of the allotment.

Visitors to Old George's allotment on a windy day all said it sounded like a yachting marina, everything clanking together, you could close your eyes and imagine you were by the sea. But, Old George didn't know anything about that... couldn't remember the last time he had been down to the coast, clapped eyes on the sea, must have been back when Amie was still alive, young Graeme, their only son, taking them to Worthing for the day, bought them a meal in an expensive restaurant, Amie and Old George both feeling uncomfortable, Amie saying she wasn't dressed for it, Graeme showing off his money, his new car, white Mercedes Saloon, electric windows, Old George saying, 'I spent five years of the war fighting those bastards, now, all you want to do is throw money at them.'

Graeme saying, 'The war's been over a long time, now, dad.'

Old George – of course, he wasn't Old George then, just plain George, 'dad' or 'pop' to Graeme – saying, 'You seen some of the things I seen, you wouldn't be so bloody anxious to forgive and forget. Germany this, Germany that... sometimes I wonder who it was did win the bloody war. Not any of the poor bastards had to fight in it, that's for sure.'

This in the fancy restaurant.

Amie saying, 'Shush, George, you're showing us up. People can hear.'

About a year before Graeme sold up, moved out to Saudi. Drawing up blueprints for public buildings, though he wasn't an architect. Old

George knew that much about what he did for a living. Spent all his free time flying out to Bangkok, God knows what he got up to out there. Old George hadn't seen his son for so long, now, he'd forgotten what he looked like.

Old George hearing the clatter of the cans, again, somebody crashing about, a voice saying, 'Fuck this for a game of soldiers.'

The Webley .38 service revolver on Old George's lap. Old George hefting its weight in two hands, standing up, pins and needles in his legs, the pain of lumbago shooting up his spine... or, perhaps, it was cancer, cancer of the prostate. He'd read somewhere that pain in the back was one of the symptoms, that and peeing blood. He had read, also, that most men had cancer of the prostate by the time they got to his age. His local GP, Dr Kooner – Indian, but, very nice, very painstaking – had told him, 'Mr Watling, prostate cancer is something you die with, not from,' prescribing a tube of Transvesin Deep Heat Rub, Old George asking Dr Kooner, Who was there to put it on for him now Amie was gone? Taking a while to work out what the doctor had meant...

About the prostate cancer.

Doctors...

What did they know?

Pushing open the shed door.

Wishing he'd oiled the hinges, bloody racket, standing in the darkness, the Webley .38 extended two-handed in front of him, saying, 'Who's there?', wondering if he should have shouted 'Freeze!' like they did in the American films...

Let whoever it was know he had a gun.

Hearing someone crashing about on his plot, brittle, hollow sound, courgette vines snapping underfoot, the last of the season before the first frost got them. A dim silhouette against the orange glow of the lights along the Richmond Road, beyond the railway embankment and the sports ground, half a mile away...

A numbing explosion in his mouth.

The salt taste of blood.

Old George's blood.

His dentures stuck half-way down his throat.

Old George on his knees...

Choking.

28

Reggie Crystal and Terry Reece-Morgan both wearing cream bath towels, Terry Reece-Morgan showing some paunch, but neither of them too bad for men in their mid-forties, the two of them lying on matching loungers beside the water in the pool room... Corney Reach Health Club, the pool room decor soft creams, big-leafed plants in terracotta pots, recessed lighting, the aquamarine of the pool shimmering off the high-vaulted ceiling and walls, the surface of the pool, a glass sheet, the pool, forty-two metres...

According to the brochure.

There was a gymnasium with cardiovascular and variable resistance machines, spa and steam bath, showers, sauna, tennis and squash courts, bar and restaurant, sun terrace, medical clinic, beauty therapy treatments and solaria.

Most important, membership was two-four-fifty per annum.

Kept out the riff-raff.

Forecourt strictly Porsche, Beamer and Mercedes. That class of motor, bottom-line.

Parking up, Reggie had spotted a Bristol, said to Terry, 'Bristol Beaumont... Tina Turner drives one of those. And that Mancunian git, sings with Oasis. Biggest band in the world, could take his pick, any woman he wanted, marries Patsy Kensit. Is that thick, or just Mancunian?'

Reggie always saying he'd had a lot of trouble with Mancunians down the years.

Terry saying, 'It takes all sorts, Reggie.'

Then: 'I wouldn't say no.'

Reggie, looking at Terry, saying, 'Hey, Terry, this is me, Reggie, you're talking to.'

Reggie, the only one called him Terry.

Not Terrance.

Right from the start.

Terry, back then saying, 'Just, for fuck's sake, don't call Rosemary "Rosy".'

Even Reggie not having the balls to do that.

Rosemary, still hating him, anyway.

Now, beside the pool, Reggie telling Terry about Corney Reach, filling him in on local history, Reggie always making a point of doing his homework before investing big money… the loop in the Thames between Hammersmith Bridge and Kew Bridge, Corney Reach, the apex of the bend, with Mortlake on the south bank. Dead Donkey Lane, the footpath cutting across the loop, been there since the sixteen hundreds, Reggie not knowing why it was called Dead Donkey Lane, but, it wasn't hard to hazard a guess. How parts of Dead Donkey Lane still existed, the walled alleyway between Chiswick Lane and Devonshire Road, the stretch of lane, just a few yards long, that ran alongside Hogarth School. Telling Terry it was all still fields a hundred years ago, Chiswick, *Cheesewicke*, dairy farm and hamlet, supplied the London markets, still a long boat-ride down river back then… How Church Street, between Hogarth Roundabout and the big money properties along Chiswick Mall was the oldest road in Chiswick…

Terry cutting in, saying, 'We're talking how many acres?'

Reggie saying, 'There's a chippy in Edensor Road, it's called The Corney Cod, would you believe?'

Then, taking the hint.

Saying: 'Pessimistically, four acres.'

'Tops?'

'Five-five.'

The two of them talking numbers, how many units at five forty-five thousand… split-level maisonettes, mock Palladian, landscaped terraces, curved driveways, keeping it spacious, all that shit.

The Burial Site.

Prime acreage.

Within spitting distance of the river.

Reggie and Terry both agreeing they should distance the project from that name.

Reggie saying, 'We have a guaranteed insight into other tenders.'

Terry laughing, saying, 'Did you fuck her... his wife, Daphne?'

Reggie saying, 'Do fuck off.'

Then: 'Any bid we enter will be viewed sympathetically.'

Then, changing the subject, feeling it was long overdue, his asking, saying, 'What news on Rosemary?'

Terry saying, 'She died twice in the ambulance, there may be brain damage.'

Reggie saying, 'I'm sorry.'

Terry saying, 'Spare me, Reggie... jumped-up little Welsh tart, isn't that how you put it?'

'There was no love lost, I'll grant you that.'

Then, Terry saying, 'I've spent all day with the accountants, and there is a problem.'

'What kind of problem?'

'Releasing money for this project.'

Reggie waiting.

Terry saying, 'Rosy has a fifty-one per cent interest in seven of the subsidiaries. In the late eighties I folded four companies, according to my accountants that now leaves Rosy with an overall controlling interest.'

'You didn't see this coming?'

'I didn't even think about it.'

'You were too generous, Terry.'

'I was in love.'

Reggie saying, 'What if she dies?'

Terry saying, 'I'll have to wait till the will is read – just like everyone else.'

Reggie saying, 'What a fucking mess.'

Then: 'What about your solicitor, didn't he advise you on this?'

Terry laughing, thinking of the condom pack, gossamer featherlite, 'Arousers', came in three flavours, slipping out of Rosy's handbag one night, her getting into the passenger seat of the Lexus, pissed... Rosy Reece, girl from the valley, strictly Chapel, with Terry it had always been lights out, missionary only, no messing.

Not her style at all.

Terry pocketing the condoms.

Not saying anything.

Not, then.

Saying to Reggie, 'Frank Gill? Expert in corporation affairs, conveyancing, ten-G retainer before he'll even roll out of bed in the morning?'

Thinking, Rosy, talking him into having the operation, vasectomy, how many years back, he couldn't remember. Rosy saying, 'You big baby, it won't hurt, not one little bit. We don't want any unwanted brats running around, getting under our feet, now, do we?'

Carrying condoms.

Featherlite.

Ribbed.

Peppermint, raspberry, chocolate.

Saying to Reggie, 'It was Frank Gill Rosy was shagging. Had somebody keeping an eye on her while I was out in Spain. Your Darren hadn't lost it when he did, I'd have been none the wiser about the contracts. The two of them could have pulled the rug right out from under me any time they wanted.'

Then: 'I'm tired of all this shit, Reggie.'

'Tired is vulnerable.'

'Tell me about it.'

Then: 'I'm going to have Darren do the bastard.'

'Frank Gill?'

'Who the fuck else?'

'I'm not sure he's up to it.'

Terry saying, 'He doesn't have a choice, Reggie.'

29

Dennis Frost, had enough of today, already, despite it was only one thirty... had enough of White Goods, had enough of Eric Dunlop bending his ear all morning, Shane sat there in the workshop listening, doing fuck all, Eric asking Dennis, What was it between Kevin and Michelle, were they back together again, or what? Dennis telling Eric, 'What the fuck is it to you? You need to know so much, go ask him yourself.'

Thinking, How come Eric Dunlop is so interested in my brother's sex life all of a sudden?

Parking up the Transit.

Hoping his mother was in, could fix him up something, fry-up, or, any luck, there would be a Balti Chicken from the supermarket she could stick in the microwave.

Chicken *ping*.

With nan bread.

Can of cold lager.

That would see him all right.

Kevin, yesterday, bottling out, deep-breathing down the telephone... dirty sod.

Last night?

After the Mason's turned out?

Don't even think about it.

Darren, on the phone this morning, Dennis telling him he hadn't torched the sheds, What was he supposed to do, turning on the mag, old geezer on his knees choking to death on his own false teeth, then throwing up, screaming blue murder?

Not telling Darren the rest... Stoney saying, 'That's it, I'm out of here, fuck the money.' Dennis deciding it had been a bad idea not offering Stoney more than twenty-five notes especially, Kevin not turning up – saying to Stoney, 'You didn't have to fucking hit him.' Stoney, like a big kid, saying, 'How did I know?' Bending over the old geezer, both of them registering the gun, Stoney, stepping back, saying, 'Oh, shit!' The old man, one leg under him, getting to his feet, one hand supporting the weight of the gun, not sure which direction to point it, coughing...

Blood dribbling down his chin.
Blinded by the mag-light.
Dennis pushing him back over.
Grabbing the gun.
Running...
Darren saying, 'No result, no money, fuck off, Dennis.'
Dennis with his key in the latch, now.
Voices from down the hall.
In the kitchen.
Dennis knowing his day could only get worse.

His mother and Jerry McNamara sitting at the kitchen table, his mother still in her dressing gown, the air thick with booze, cigarette smoke, and something else Dennis didn't recognise: two lines of what Dennis thought must be cocaine on the formica table-top, Dennis saying to his mother, 'Christ, you still in your dressing gown... this time of day?'

Jerry, smiling, saying, 'And good morning to you, too, Dennis.'

Jerry McNamara.
His mother's new flame.
Feet under the table, already.
Saying to Dennis, 'You're just in time.'
Looking towards the two lines on the table.
Dennis saying, 'I don't do coke.'
Then, to his mother, 'Any chance of something to eat?'
Thinking, fat chance.
Seeing her eyes.
Completely out of it.
Jerry saying, 'Yuppy dust? Do me a favour.'
Handing Dennis a straw.

McDonald's Thick Shake.

Saying, 'Give it a try... one line of this you could run all the way to Brighton and back, not stopping.'

Pat, his mother, saying, 'I can make you a sandwich?'

Dennis saying, 'Don't bother, I'll get something down the road... something hot.'

Jerry saying, 'Crystal meth.'

'What?'

'Crank... you want to try some.'

Not a question.

A statement.

His mother, pushing back her chair, but not standing up, saying, 'I'll put a kettle on.'

Dennis saying, 'Don't fucking bother.'

Jerry saying, 'You shouldn't swear in front of your mother.'

Dennis thinking what he had said to Stoney, last night in The Mason's Arms, while they were hanging on, seeing if Kevin was going to turn up, Dennis telling Stoney that all he really wanted to do was to go to New Zealand...

Stoney saying, 'New Zealand? Why New Zealand?'

Dennis saying, 'Because it's about as far from here as you can fucking get.'

The two of them at the bar, Ted taking his time pulling Dennis a Guinness, Ted saying, 'All right, if you're into sheep shagging.'

Then: 'I bet you don't even know the capital?'

Dennis saying, 'Auckland.'

Right off the top of his head.

None of them, including Dennis, sure if Dennis was right.

Dennis saying to Jerry, 'Oh? Really?'

Pat, seeing where this was heading.

Looking to diffuse the situation, saying, 'I'm missing *Neighbours*.'

Dennis, knowing she never watched it this time of day.

Not, ever.

His mother reaching across to the TV, black and white portable on the kitchen sideboard, came free with the colour rental, turning the volume up loud, moving her chair round, half facing the screen.

Dennis thinking, Why not Australia? Why does it have to be New Zealand?

Lou Carpenter giving Toadfish a hard time... Helen Daniels, boring as ever, why the fuck hadn't she pegged, that last stroke she had?

Everything cold and gloomy in black and white.

Jerry doing the two lines.

Dennis going upstairs to his bedroom.

Opening the top drawer of the dresser.

The old man's gun wrapped in a black T-shirt.

The Stranglers.

How the fuck long had he had *that* T-shirt?

Going back downstairs, pointing the gun in Jerry's face, saying, 'Get the fuck out of my house, right now.'

30

The young man pushed in through the double plate-glass doors of the pool room, smiled at Reggie and Terry. Terry, seeing the look on Reggie's face, saying, 'Now, is not the right time for this.'

Reggie saying, 'A little relaxation… take your mind off your problems. Call it a home-coming present.'

Then: 'His name is Karl. His father is a German industrialist, has a place along the river, opposite Chiswick Eyot. Karl gets bored easily.'

The boy was tall, stooped shoulders, trying to disguise his height, long face, milky blue eyes… Terry, later, discovering his balls, fat flat ovals, discus, his prick, medium-sized, thin, circumcised. Watching, now, as the boy dropped his towel, plunged into the pool, began swimming lengths.

Crawl.

Later, kissing, fondling the boy, treating Karl as if he was a woman.

Karl saying, 'I don't kiss.'

Then: 'Lay back.'

Cupping Terry in his hands, both hands, holding his prick as if Terry was a frightened bird, about to fly away.

Then freeing one hand.

Grasping Terry with the other.

Pumping.

Finding a handkerchief, somewhere, for Terry to spill into…

Terry hating that.

Hating it, also, when Karl said, 'Did you enjoy that? Was it good?'

Perfect English.
Terry, lying, saying, 'Vonderbar.'
V not W.
Not much of a joke.
Not much of a wank, either.
Terry thinking, No, not wank.
Vank.
Then thinking, Just because I like boys…
Doesn't make me a dick-breath.

31

Grace, by the boating lake in Gunnersbury Park, sitting with the two men, one of them saying to Grace, 'You're all right, missy.' The two of them drinking from the neck, passing back and forth the 75cl bottle of Cutty Sark; Grace, when she had sat down on the bench, earlier, the bottle of whisky still in a Thresher's brown paper carrier-bag, saying, 'Here... this is for you.'

One of the men saying, 'All of it?'

Looking in the carrier-bag.

Expecting a trick.

Then, saying, 'You don't want any?'

Grace, saying, 'I don't want any.'

Thinking, Bloody liar.

Across the lake the Autumn wind was blowing the first leaves from the trees. There was a snap in the air, despite the sun. The cafe and ice cream kiosk had closed till Spring. In South Ealing Road a tobacconist and newsagent had a sign in his window which he amended every day. This morning, it read: ONLY 80 MORE SHOPPING DAYS TO CHRISTMAS!

Grace, thinking, Eighty days?

That seemed like forever.

Remembering when there used to be boats on the lake.

Before the two kids drowned.

A brother and sister.

One Sunday afternoon, the park crowded, you'd have thought somebody would have noticed.

One of the men on the bench, the one next to Grace, nudging her with his elbow, saying, 'I don't suppose you fancy a shag, missy?'

Grace saying, 'Thank you, no.'
Nudging her, again.
'You can't blame a feller for asking, now, can you?'
Grace telling him, No, she couldn't.
The man saying, 'No offence, missy.'
Grace saying, 'None taken.'

She had bought the Cutty Sark to celebrate putting the house on the market. The representative from the estate agency, Dewhurst & Spink in Northfield Avenue, had come to view the house, recommending an asking price of one hundred and thirty-two thousand pounds.

Grace couldn't imagine what it would be like to actually *have* that amount of money.

Saying to the estate agent's representative, 'Does that include the Ford Cortina Estate?'

Stoney's Cortina 2.00 GL, X Registration.

Still up on blocks in the front garden.

Leaking engine oil onto the crazy paving.

The estate agent's representative had laughed, young and confident, perfectly but conservatively dressed, good fortune still his birthright, his car out on the road, red and gleaming chrome.

Thinking Grace was joking.

She had seen Stoney, from a distance, in the park at the weekend, over on the sports field playing football with a bunch of kids.

Stoney, off in a world of his own.

Cantona.

Ryan Giggs.

Shearer...

Who knows?

The kids shouting, 'Pass the ball, mister... *pass* the ball!'

Grace wondering how much he missed her.

Could it be as much as she missed him?

Looking at her companions, the two men on the bench, the bottle of Cutty Sark almost finished, thinking, Is this what you want? Is this what you really want?

Then, thinking, But Christ, do they look happy.

32

Duncan having trouble seeing over the heads of the crowd, feeling trapped, hemmed in, as if he had been swallowed and eaten alive by the gyrating throng... feeling old. Saying to Carol when they arrived, Carol's name, plus one, on the guest list, 'How come half the audience is wearing floppy, wide-brimmed leather hats? Is that retro or post-modernist hippy?' Making a joke, having to shout in Carol's ear to be heard. Carol saying, 'Somebody over there I *have* to speak to... back in a mo'.'

Three numbers...

Half an hour... ago.

Duncan's glass empty, wanting to get to the bar, another pint of Young's Special – how many was that? – concerned that he would lose Carol if he moved. Deciding he would wait till he needed another pee.

Two birds.

One stone.

Catching a glimpse of the lead singer.

Long blond hair in the spotlight.

The band called Mojo Spliff.

Changed their name from Muse-ik.

On the green that lunchtime, Duncan eating pastrami with pickle on rye, Carol eating walnut and avocado, baguette roll, Carol saying, 'A declaration of the importance of the muse in music... at the same time, Muse-ik? Muzak? There's a subtle irony there, don't you think?'

Duncan saying, 'Why on earth should they have wanted to change their name?'

Carol saying, 'It was sending out a wrong message. People thought they were techno.'

'Heaven forbid.'

Duncan's own subtle ironies going unnoticed.

Saying, 'We won't be doing much more of this.'

'How do you mean?'

'Winter coming on... it will be too cold soon.'

Missing, in advance, the intimacy of their lunches on the green... a wine bar, crowded pub, it wouldn't be the same. Duncan frightened that their relationship was about to take a step backwards.

Carol saying, 'Why don't you come, tonight? They're playing in Putney?'

Duncan, taken by surprise, saying, 'Oh, I don't know.'

Wondering what the invitation meant.

Carol saying, 'You need cheering up... take your mind off your noisy neighbours.'

'Don't remind me of that bitch.'

'Not *black* bitch?'

'Carol, you know me better than that.'

'My... we are improving.'

Letters to the Office of the Environment.

Noise pollution.

The latest salvo...

Saying, 'I really don't need you patronising me, Carol.'

Carol saying, 'Do say you'll come... go on.'

Her hand reaching out across the grass.

Touching his knee.

That afternoon, ringing Lindsay at work... CSA, Chief Executive's Office, Lindsay one of a team of four, Lindsay coming on the line, saying, 'Oh, it's you. Makes a change from the usual irate fathers, impoverished mothers, confused MPs, and secretaries of state who seem to hold me personally responsible whenever we get bad press.' Then: 'A gig? Duncan, you don't even *like* music.' Having no doubt in her mind, not, what the invitation meant, rather, what Duncan might think it meant.

Hoping he wasn't about to make a fool of himself. Saying, 'I'll bang on my own till you get back.'

Duncan saying, 'What?'
'The wall.'
'Oh...'
Then: 'Lindsay, if you don't want me to go?'
Lindsay saying, 'Go... enjoy.'
Duncan now thinking, Enjoy?
Enjoy what?
Feeling old?
Pissed?
Infatuated with a young girl half his age?

The band thanking their audience. Saying, This would have to be the last number. Duncan thinking, Promises, promises. Aware that Carol was back beside him, saying to her, 'So, how will you review the gig?'

Carol, up close to his ear, saying, 'Good, melodic Indie Pop, the power of the songs diluted by an amateurish presentation which betrays their folk roots. Mojo Spliff need more confidence in their own material.'

Then: 'What do you think?'
'I'm impressed.'
'No, the band?'
'Well, I must confess, I'm relieved this is their last number.'
'Don't you believe it... there'll be two encores, at least.'
The two of them pushed together by the crowd.

Duncan aware of her body against his... the movement of her hips, was that intentional? His hands reaching behind, caressing her buttocks, Carol saying, 'Duncan, what are you doing?'

Pulling away.
Then: 'Oh, God! I've been so silly.'

33

Darren's first big mistake.

Falling asleep when they were playing Who Moves First. Fast asleep... still erect, deep inside her, Darren's mouth open next to her ear, snoring, Kiren saying, 'Okay, Angel Face, you win.'

Easing out from under him.

Thinking, sometimes, when you win you lose.

Bringing herself off.

Too pissed with Darren to go find a vibrator.

Darren's second big mistake was the next evening, around seven-thirty, Kiren wanting to go out to a Greek restaurant, Adamou's, the wrong end of the Bayswater Road, everybody raving about the place, Tara and Tamara both seen eating there in the same week... you went through to the kitchen, picked your food from what was on the stove, like in a real Greek restaurant.

Kiren saying, 'Sounds great fun.'

Wanting to show off the Daniel Herschen hair and manicure, simple *chignon*, nails... the new Chanel metal-shot claret... military-style overcoat, Harrods, The Coat Room, First Floor, she could wear it now the nights were colder.

Wanting to feel good.

Despite Darren was now living on another planet.

Darren saying, 'Real Greek restaurant?'

Thinking, Reggie's 'up-front' money down to a low three figures, the Jaguar on borrowed time, did he really need this?

Saying, 'You think there are any *real* Greek restaurants left in Greece?'

Remembering, once, Reggie telling him about a Greek restaurant you picked your own food, the Greek quarter, Bonn. Just a house. You ate in the living room, Granny there with her feet up watching television. Afterwards, the son running down the road, refusing to take the tip they had left, saying, It was an honour. Reggie saying it was the best Greek food he ever had...

Germany.

Reggie going through one of his phases.

Encouraging Darren to travel.

See the world.

Darren thinking, Why the fuck should I go see the world... wait long enough the whole fucking world will be right here in London?

Saying, now, to Kiren, 'I hate Greek restaurants... I hate Greeks. It was a Greek killed The King, did you know that? His personal physician, Dr George Nichopolous. They found fourteen different drugs in Elvis's body... Demerol, Elavil, Codeine, Morphine, Valium, Methaqualone.'

Kiren saying, 'That's only six.'

Darren saying, 'Don't get clever with me, Kiren.'

Then: 'Eighteen cardiovascular experts tried to revive him. The County Medical Examiner certified him dead at 3.30 pm... Cardiac Arrhythmia.'

Then: 'August Sixteen.'

Then: '...Nineteen Seventy-Seven.'

Kiren saying, 'You're losing it, Darren.'

Darren saying, 'Memphis Baptist Memorial Hospital, Trauma Room Two.'

Then: 'Did you ever wonder who was in Trauma Room One the afternoon The King died?'

Kiren saying, 'Darren, you are a sad crazy fuck. No, correct that, you're not even a fuck, any more. I want you out of my flat. I'm going out. I'm eating Greek. By the time I get back, I want you gone.'

'Now, call me a cab.'

Darren saying, 'Kiren?'

Kiren saying, 'Don't go pathetic on me, I'd hate to have to call the police.'

34

Stoney and Mrs M getting on like a house on fire, Stoney going downstairs for tea and sandwiches, chocolate cup cakes, every afternoon at four-thirty sharp, the sandwiches either ham and tomato or cheese and pickle on medium white sliced... sometimes, toasted crumpets with marmite instead of the sandwiches.

Mrs M saying to Stoney every day while she was clearing the plates, 'A good inside stomach lining never did hurt anybody... you should take a bit more care of yourself.'

And: 'Nice looking young man like you, it's about time you found yourself a wife, someone to look after you.'

Nice looking?

Young man?

Stoney loving every minute of it.

Saying, 'If you were only twenty years younger, Mrs M.'

Mrs M saying, 'Get away with you, you cheeky young bugger.'

The house in Banham Street.

Stoney, the upstairs flat.

Mrs M downstairs...

Had lived there forty years, ever since they built the new road and Hammersmith Flyover, knocked down the house where she used to live with her husband, Billy, before he was killed on the Rhine, last months of the war... where she gave birth to her only daughter, Katherine, she in her turn dying with her husband, Richard, and their two young girls, Sam and Ellie, plane crash, 1971, Yugoslavia.

Their first holiday abroad.

Mrs M kept the postcard on the mantlepiece next to a sepia studio photograph of Billy in uniform, before he was drafted overseas: WEATHER LOVELY, FOOD AWFUL. SAM AND ELLIE SPEND THEIR WHOLE DAY IN THE WATER... SEE YOU NEXT WEEK, LOVE AND LOTS OF KISSES, KATH, RICHARD, SAM AND ELLIE.

Sam, four.

Ellie, seven.

Mrs M saying to Stoney, 'I'd told them, when they said they were going, "Sooner, you than me... you'll never catch me up in one of those things".'

Then: 'I never dreamed.'

The postcard arriving after the news.

The policeman and the WPC standing on the doorstep, the WPC saying, 'Mrs Moynihan? Would you mind if we come in?'

Mrs M's name.

Moynihan.

Stoney saying, 'You've had a life, haven't you?'

Mrs M saying, 'I was living here by then... moved in '55. The plane crash was in '71. Katherine was thirty-five when she died, would have been sixty-one by now, the girls both in their thirties... doesn't seem possible, does it?'

Then: 'Still, at least, they had a nice holiday before they went.'

Stoney never sure when Mrs M was joking.

Old people.

Who could understand them?

Mrs M saying all her happiest memories were in the old house, Verbena Gardens... told Stoney, if it was ever on the telly again, you could catch a glimpse of Verbena Gardens, how it looked before they built the new road, in that film, *The Cockleshell Heroes* – Trevor Howard was the star, he used to live in Verbena Gardens, always throwing empty whiskey bottles through his front room window, must have been why they picked it – there is a scene where this young commando comes home on a forty-eight hour pass, catches his wife with another bloke, chucks him out of the house... you can see Verbena Gardens, clear as anything, in the background.

Happiest memories.

Her years with her husband, Billy.

Katherine, born in the back bedroom, Mrs M in labour for eleven hours, the doctor wanting to get her into hospital, Mrs M having none of it...

Billy chain-smoking in the kitchen.

Player's Weights.

Husbands weren't allowed to be present at the delivery back in those days.

Mrs M saying to Stoney, 'You know, I've never so much as looked at another man, since.'

Then: 'Silly bugger, I told him, thirty-six he was, when he joined up, couldn't wait to get down to the recruitment office.

'Me with Katherine barely out of nappies.

'Leaving us all alone like that.'

Mrs M in the kitchen, running water for the washing-up, saying to Stoney, 'And, now, they want to move me out of here... young man from the rent office was round, telling me I ought to consider sheltered accommodation. Asking me if I didn't think it might not be a good idea, what with the arthritis, and everything.'

Stoney pushing back his chair, standing up, Mrs M saying, 'You don't have to go, just because I'm started tidying up.'

Stoney saying, 'What did you say... to this bloke came round?'

Wanting to leave.

Dying for a cigarette.

Mrs M very strict about nobody smoking in her flat.

Mrs M saying, 'I told him I was too old to think about moving, that I was quite happy where I was, thank you very much.'

'What did he say to that?'

'He left me some brochures, said I should think about it... one of those cocky young buggers, won't take "no" for an answer.'

Stoney saying, 'Well, you let me know if he starts bothering you.'

'I've already told him, with that nice young Mr Todd upstairs to keep an eye out for me, why should I be troubling my head with ideas about sheltered housing?'

Stoney thinking, It was a pity Grace wasn't here.

She was good with the old folks.

Never patronising… not like those fucking social workers always round to see his old man when he wasn't in hospital. Showing him no respect, calling him by his first name, Stoney's old man saying, 'Have we met? Do I know you from somewhere? It's Mr Todd to you, and don't you forget it.'

Same way Grace treated kids.

Like people in their own right. Assuming they had a past…

And a future.

Stoney saying, 'You'll have to meet my Grace, sometime.'

'Your Grace?'

Coming in from the scullery.

'My wife, Grace.'

Mrs M saying, 'Sit down… I'll put another kettle on, you can tell me all about her.'

Stoney, wishing he had never mentioned Grace, saying, 'I don't suppose it's all right to smoke, just this once.'

Mrs M saying, 'You suppose right.'

35

The first thing Monica did after she decided for certain that Kevin was back shagging his ex-wife, Michelle, was to pour the entire content of a bottle of Absolut Vodka into his beloved marine fish tank.

Emperor angels, triggers, pufferfish, scorpions, wrasse, mandarins, damsels, clowns... all swimming frenetically, going into spasm, the wrasse – rainbow wrasse, Kevin had said it was... he was particularly fond of the rainbow wrasse diving into the coral sand at the bottom of the tank, each fish, in its own time, stiffening in a final spasm and floating to the surface.

Anemones closing up.

Brown blobs on the white coral clusters.

Invertebrates, boxer shrimp, cleaner shrimp, circulating lifelessly in the current created by the Kiho air pump and under-gravel filtration system.

Michelle knowing all the names.

Twelve months, Kevin had been boring her senseless on the subject.

Turning off the Kiho air pump.

The silence.

Bliss.

Stoney saying to her, earlier, when he had popped round, let himself in with a key, still hadn't remembered to give it back, 'To wet the baby's head... just a thank you for putting up with me.'

Giving Monica the bottle of Absolut.

'A pressy.'

Monica saying, 'Stoney, you shouldn't have... really.' Had

been about to say, 'You might have knocked.' Feeling guilty at the way she had always treated him. Hardly, the gracious hostess.

Stoney asking, Where's Kevin and How's Kevin? Monica not saying that she had decided in her head that he was back screwing Michelle, probably at it that very moment. Instead saying she thought Kevin might be cracking up. Telling Stoney, that very morning, before going off to the garage, he had said to Monica, 'If it's a boy, we should call it Duane.'

Stoney saying, 'Duane?'

Monica saying, 'Exactly what I said.'

Thinking, It will be a girl.

Scarlet.

Scarlet James.

James, Monica's maiden name.

Stoney, not comfortable with it being just the two of them, saying, 'Well…'

Then, 'Tell Kevin I called in, won't you?'

At the front door, saying, 'Now, I'm in Hammersmith, don't see so much of the lads… like ships that pass in the wind.'

Monica thinking, Ships that pass in the wind?

Saying, 'Oh, Stoney.'

Remembering Kevin and Dennis at the kitchen table one night, something Stoney had said, earlier, in the Mason's, Kevin and Dennis laughing hysterically. Kevin, quoting Stoney, saying, 'Bruce Oldfield… wasn't he one of the Barnaby Boys?'

Bruce Oldfield.

Fashion designer.

Working class lad, made good.

Stoney meaning, Dr Bernado's.

Then, Dennis, coming in with, 'Big Chef?'

Which had them pissing themselves.

Big Chief.

Little Chef.

Kevin and Dennis howling… Monica thinking, And these are Stoney's friends?

Asha-dejar.

Déjà vu.

Saying, again, 'Oh, Stoney.'

Back in the front room, the wall clock reading seven fifteen, Kevin's pork chops and macaroni cheese dried out in the oven, Kevin taking a shower this morning before he went off to work.

Motor mechanic?

Showering in the morning?

Telling Monica he would be popping in to Michelle's, Kitty's birthday, had to drop her round a present.

Monica thinking, Oh fuck off, Kevin!

Thinking, Is this how Michelle felt when I was shagging Kevin behind *her* back? Whatever goes around, comes round... never too sure what that meant.

Till now.

Staring at the fish tank. Watching the scorpion fish stalk a live shrimp... the live shrimp there one second, gone the next, swallowed whole in a movement too fast for the eye to follow.

Kevin saying, 'Look... you never see it happen.'

Monica saying, 'So, what's the point?'

Just a swirl of disturbed sand.

Kevin saying, 'Telescopic mouth.'

Monica thinking, watching the scorpion fish rising through the water, fan-tailed plumage wafting in the current, smug, satisfied, 'Right, fucker, you are dead meat.'

36

Kiren in a black cab, decided on Claridges for breakfast, eggs Benedict, bacon and muffins, why shouldn't she spoil herself after last night, her wrists still painful, Darren being such an absolute pig?

The phone waking her this morning, Kiren thinking it would be Darren. Her mother, Dorothy, calling from Burundi, saying, 'Did I wake you?'

Kiren saying, 'Mother?'

Half asleep.

Hung over.

Thinking she was ringing about Darren.

Realising, How could she possibly know?

Her mother telling Kiren about the Italian Count she had meet, 'Genuine aristocrat', in Rwanda as part of a fact-finding mission for the UN, special brief on the returning Hutus, had invited her to Milan for Christmas. Kiren not remembering the last time her mother had sounded this animated... this excited. Her mother saying, 'Imagine, darling, *all* my favourite watering holes. Il Fondaco Dei Mori, Osteria Del Pallone, The Four Seasons. And the shopping... rather long in the tooth for Dolce and Gabbana – I do prefer to wear my corsetry on the inside – but, I'm sure I'll find some consolation.' Vetrina Di Beryl, Cammarata, Anteprima, Prada, '...and, of course, there's always Via Ripamonti on a Sunday morning.'

Kiren thinking about last night, back from Adamou's, an act of defiance that she should go alone, drunk on Retsina and Metaxas Brandy, grateful that Darren's car had disappeared, that he wasn't at the flat when she got home... meeting Helen on the doorstep, chauffeur waiting at the curb with a limousine, Helen dressed to kill, off to meet one of her regular clients. Kiren wondering how it would feel to be paid for sex, remembering that writer, in one of the Sunday's, made a big thing of doing it for a set of Le Creuset. Kiren deciding her body was worth rather more than a set of saucepans, even if they were Le Creuset.

Anyway, what on earth could one do with a set of saucepans?

Cook?

Helen asking if she was all right.

Heard the row, earlier, through the ceiling.

Kiren saying, 'Yes, fine... absolutely.'

Saying, this morning, to her mother, 'You are sounding incredibly buoyant, I must say, mother. We're through our austerity and self-sacrificial phase, are we?'

Kiren's mother saying, 'What?'

Born of an age and a class where Excuse me? or Pardon? were considered *déclassé*.

'You've dumped the hair shirt.'

Her mother laughing, saying, 'Amazing the effect of a good rogering, don't you think?'

Kiren saying, 'Mother!'

Not willing to think of her in that way.

Not mentioning Darren.

After the call, showering, dressing, deciding she would spend the day as a tourist in her own city. Bond Street, Sloane Street... Armani, Versace, Missoni, Valentino, who needed a flight to Milan, she could pick up a Gucci hoover bag – how *de rigueur*, my dear – right here in London.

The cab stuck in traffic, South Audley Street. Grosvenor Square, bleak in the drizzle, office workers with their golfing umbrellas the only splash of colour in a grey morning... her mother coming to Grosvenor Square, long before Kiren was born, CND demonstrations, Committee of 100, embarrassing her father, a group-captain by then, the two of them already at Windcroft, still a couple. Kiren seeing the scene in black and white, imagining the square full of young people, duffel coats, long hair, her mother one of those young people. The cabby, earlier, when he picked her up outside Ladbroke Grove Station, beneath the shelter of the railway bridge, saying, 'You'd be better off on the tube this time of day... what with the rain.'

Adding, 'Missy.'

Kiren, saying, 'I'm in no hurry.'

The cabby saying, 'All right for some.'

Saying to Kiren, now, pulling back the glass divider, gesturing towards the traffic, not moving, around Grosvenor Square, 'Don't say I didn't warn you.'

Portable radio on the dash.

Capital Gold.

Caught in a trap, I can't get back,
You know I love you too much, baby...

Darren singing that same song last night, grabbing her wrists, holding them tight, Kiren saying, 'Let go, you bastard, you're hurting me.' Darren saying, 'I can't remember the last time I felt this angry.'

But, not looking angry.

That frightened Kiren most.

Darren not *looking* angry.

Kiren, leaning forward, saying to the cabby, 'Would you mind? I'd rather not have the music.'

Darren singing:

'*Why can't you see, what you're doing to me,*
I can't believe a word you're saying...'

His hand enclosing one of Kiren's fingers, forcing the finger in on itself, saying, 'Snap!'

Then: 'Only joking.'

Then: 'Don't pig out on the souvlaka.'

Kiren not seeing it coming, her cheek stinging from the open-handed slap, saying, screaming, 'You fucking bastard! You're a psycho, you know that?'

Darren saying, 'Psycho? As in psychopath... somebody else called me that, once.'

Kiren screaming, 'I don't need to hear this!'

Darren saying, 'I looked it up – you know, those words you *think* you know what they mean till it comes to it? "Person suffering chronic mental disorder, a mentally or emotionally disturbed person", learned it by heart, *The Concise Oxford*

Dictionary. Nowhere did it say anything about being dangerous. You like that, don't you, Kiren... dangerous?'

Kiren, now, saying to the cabby, 'Here will do fine,' handing him a ten and a five, saying, 'No, that's all right.'

Walking across Grosvenor Square.

Along Brook Street.

Feeling self-conscious.

Because of Darren, wearing dark glasses in the rain.

Saying, last night, 'Darren, you are not funny.'

Darren saying, 'Who's laughing?'

37

Alison and Darren in Alison's flat, glass of Rumanian Red and a spliff – Whacky Backy, Darren called it, reminiscing on the good old days of Class Act, Alison saying, 'Well, you know what they say about the good old days, they're only good after they've gone.'

Darren saying, 'Eddie? How's he doing with the new place?'

Double-frontage.

Goldhawk Road.

Still had Ms Joy-fucking-Shanks from the VAT Office on the phone daily, asking after Darren.

Alison saying, 'You know Eddie.'

Darren, passing the spliff to Alison, saying, 'This stuff never did do much for me.'

Then: 'Hardly a bundle of laughs.'

Meaning Eddie.

Alison's flat, two rooms, kitchen and bathroom, above a butcher's shop in Bollo Bridge Road, Chiswick end of Acton, Jimmy the Butcher been there thirty years, man and boy, still cut his meat from the carcass, telling Alison he was going to retire once the lease was up for renewal, saying, 'Don't see much point, all my profit going to the landlord…

'…he sits there on his fat arse.'

Alison telling Darren, all she could hear of Jimmy the Butcher, when she was home during the day, or, on Saturdays, was the sound of Jimmy's meat cleaver going *thwack* into the chopping block… carrying up through the ceiling.

Jimmy saying he had been offered a fortune for that chopping block, concave, cross-hatched from years of service. Jimmy saying, 'It's a mystery to me, what people are willing to spend their money on…'

And: 'More money than sense, most of them.'

Alison, vegetarian since childhood, with every reverberation of Jimmy the Butcher's meat cleaver through the ceiling, imagining the dividing of dull red meat.

The splintering of bone.

The paring of flesh.

Saying to Darren, 'I'll miss Jimmy, but, I'm not going to miss that bloody meat cleaver.'

Pouring more red wine.

The two of them on the settee in the living room, Moroccan throw, holiday two years back, covering the settee, bright yellows and reds, black silhouettes of dancing figures, Darren saying, watching Alison roll a third spliff, 'I can't look at that too long, I really can't.'

Both laughing.

Alison talking about the surcharges.

Hidden extras.

Darren saying, 'Ten per cent for a double-barrel, ten per cent if they called their house a property, ten per cent for saying, "My daily will have the key."' Alison giggling, saying, 'You remember her… "My daily who comes in twice a week," all of us losing it, even Eddie couldn't keep a straight face.' Both of them, tears running down their cheeks, now, Darren wiping his eyes, saying, 'Ten per cent for Bedford Park Border,' meaning South Acton, ten per cent for close to the river, twenty-five per cent for actually *on* the river, plus seventeen and a half per cent VAT.'x

Alison howling.

Saying, 'VAT… as in Very Awful Type.'

'That woman on the TV, looks like she's had a stroke, one side of her face all crooked…?'

'Anne Robinson?'

'In one… Anne Robinson, *Watchdog*. Can you imagine, "This week we shall be investigating the hidden cost of double-glazing."'

'Wagging her finger at the screen.'

'Like somebody's maiden aunt.'
Which set the two of them off, again.
Then Alison, saying, 'We had some fun.'
Darren saying, 'Too fucking right, we did.'
Then: 'What happened, Alison?'

Alison saying, 'Don't go maudlin on me, Darren. What happened was Class Act had a cash flow problem as in you couldn't keep your hand out of the till... that, and collecting government taxes on your own behalf.'

'But, it was my business, my money.'

Contrite.

Childlike.

'Your problem was, Darren, you could never tell gross from net.'

Then: 'You still don't get it, do you?'

Darren rolling his pupils up into his eye sockets, falling towards Alison on the settee. Alison, laughing, saying, 'You daft bugger.' Darren biting her ear, his hand coming round to her breast, no bra, Alison saying, 'I don't think this is a very good idea.'

Removing Darren's hand.

Standing up.

Darren saying, 'But, there's only the one bed?'

Smiling.

Still not given up hope.

Alison saying, 'You're on the settee... and it's just the one night.'

'One night?'

Alison repeating: 'One night.'

Part Five
Sorted…

Duncan could not remember ever feeling quite this tired before – imagined this was how it would feel when he was an old man. An old man who could dismiss his current forty-nine years as the last bloom of youth. An old man who had outlived all his loved ones, all his friends. Duncan thinking, What loved ones? What friends? Sitting on the first step of the hallway stairs, leaning into the balustrade. Knowing with absolute certainty, no matter how hard he tried, he would be unable to get to his feet, climb the stairs, wash, undress, crawl into bed... put an end to this whole disastrous evening.

His crutch warm... damp.
Memories of childhood.
Wetting the bed.
Warm.
Then, cold.
Duncan thinking, had he peed himself?
Was he that drunk?
Dropping Carol at her house, Sheen Lane, off Lower Richmond Road, leaving the engine running, saying nothing. Carol, not moving, saying, 'Why don't you leave the car here? I'll call you a cab, we can have a coffee.'
Duncan saying, 'I'll be fine.'
Turning the key in the ignition.
Engine, still running, shrieking, Duncan saying, 'Oh, sod!'
Carol saying, 'You really shouldn't be driving.'
Duncan saying, 'I'll be all right!'
The three door F Reg Fiat Panda... small, grey, undistinguished, not likely to solicit the attentions of the police unless he was driving badly.
Which he was not.
Saying, 'If you think this is a skinful...' Knowing, as he spoke, that he sounded like a boastful first year college student.
How much was it, anyway?
Five pints?
Six?
Two shorts at the bar as they were closing.
Or, was it three?
Carol saying to the bar staff, 'We're with the band,' wanting to

hang around, chat to the musicians when they came down from the dressing room. Duncan not recognising them at first, mixing with friends, relatives, hangers-on, divest of their stage clothes, away from the stage lights... having a sudden, overdue insight into the theatricality of it all.

Saying, now, to Carol, 'I should say I'm sorry.'
Carol saying, 'No, Duncan, it's me who should be saying sorry.'
Duncan laughing.
Saying, 'But, neither of us actually saying it.'
Carol saying, 'Oh, Duncan.'
Duncan saying, 'Sorry.'
Waiting for Carol to get out of the car.
Reaching across, having to undo his seat-belt first, winding down the off-side window, saying, 'Our ages... a relationship. It would hardly be a precedent.'
Carol saying, 'Age? It isn't an age thing. I just don't fancy you.'
Adding: 'I can't help that... sorry.'
Duncan saying, 'See? That wasn't so hard.'
'What?'
'Sorry.'
Carol saying, 'Christ! You can be a facetious sod.'
Then: 'Our lunch-time scenes... I don't see they are such a good idea, not after tonight.'
Duncan falling forward, toppling slowly, surprised at the impact when he hit the floor, face to the carpet, head turned sideways, he could see the front door, feel the draft coming under the door, the narrow gap between the door and the sill.
His mouth salty.
Dribbling.
Lindsay?
Where was Lindsay?
A sudden, massive fire in his abdomen.
Throwing up.
Not sick...
Blood.
Crossing the Thames, at Mortlake, the fast two-lane stretch between Chiswick Bridge, over the river, and the Great Chertsey Road Railway Bridge, moving from one lane to the other, not sure which lane he wanted to be in, knowing the road would narrow to one lane on

the bend, then widen out again... not wanting to clip the curb, afraid he might veer into oncoming traffic. Indicating left, coming up to the lights, junction with Sutton Court Road, level with the Old Burial Site, the Crematorium, the allotments... across the road, Chiswick School. The Fiat not wanting to make the turn into Sutton Court Road, Duncan surprised at his speed.

Hitting the bollard.

The wheel torn from his hands, the car careering across Sutton Court Road, deep grooves in the grass verge, colliding with the wall, the base of the tree.

Avenue of poplars.

Duncan thinking, Just like they used to have everywhere in France... except they had white bands painted round them.

A warning to motorists.

The car motionless.

Tick-tock of the cooling engine.

Duncan seeing the frosted windscreen, feeling the weight of the steering wheel against his stomach, the car seat jammed forward on its runners. Thinking, This is okay. This is not a disaster. Sutton Court Road, Falconberg Road, five minutes, I'm home.

Sort out the car tomorrow.

Surprised when the car door opened.

That he could stand.

An ocean of blood.

Deep dark red.

This was the hallway?

This was the hallway carpet?

Lindsay would go crazy.

...hearing the music before he had turned the corner, thinking, Final stretch. The avenue of poplars, the avenue of cherry. Lindsay always making a point of telling him, every spring, when the cherries came into blossom. Seeing the two men up ahead blocking the pavement, the girl next door at her open window, leaning out, shouting at them, her words lost to the pounding bass rhythms.

Ragga reggae.

Duncan knew about reggae.

Carol had explained the ragga.

Why was nobody complaining?

The two men, both black, in their early twenties. One of them *wearing a snow-white kagoul, USA and the Stars and Stripes on the front. The other, black bomber jacket, tan T-shirt, white designer jeans, both of them with shaved heads. Duncan not even scared... feeling good. Life had offered him a second chance.*

He was invincible.

Saying, 'Neil Sedaka? I bet you never heard of Neil Sedaka? Real music, tunes with melodies?'

Singing:

Oh, Carol, I am but a fool,
Darling, I love you,
But you treat me cruel.

Stumbling into the two men.

The smell of tobacco.

The girl upstairs laughing.

Feeling the sharp, gut-wrenching pain.

Now, the fear. A fear so profound it robbed Duncan of breath... that bitch-from-hell next door, that black *bitch-from-hell next door... Duncan, on the Green, saying to Carol, 'If she was fat, I'd call her a fat bitch -*

'Wouldn't I?'

At least, the music had stopped.

Hearing the door, Lindsay's voice.

'Oh, dear! Oh, dear!'

Then: 'Oh, dear! Oh, dear! Oh, dear!'

Duncan thinking, How many 'Oh, dears' does it take to crowd out a room, leave you having to tread all over the body?

Knowing it made no sense.

38

The young girl behind the desk in the travel agency saying to Grace, 'Hi! I'm Sara. How may I be of assistance?' Pronouncing 'Sara'.

As in tiara.

Offering Grace the seat in front of her desk.

Grace sitting down.

Thinking, Sara?

As, in tiara?

Sara reading Grace's thoughts, saying, 'It's without the H.' Pointing at the laminate on her blouse. The laminate reading: SARA CUSSON, TRAVEL ADVISER, SUNSCOPE HOLIDAYS. Beneath that, in smaller print: AITO/ATOL.

Grace, thinking of Japanese names and Pacific atolls, no idea what that last part meant, saying, 'Goodness, the difference an H can make.'

Sunscope Holidays.

On Acton High Street, across the road from the church and the Tesco Supermarket, single shop front between The Home Brew Emporium, went bust within six months – EXPERTS TO HELP AND ADVISE! BEAT THE TAX MAN! BREW THE BEER OF YOUR CHOICE HERE ON THE PREMISES! – and the Standard Indian Restaurant.

Been there forever.

When Grace's father's money came through, Grace took Stoney to the Standard to celebrate. They had been going there regularly ever since, Grace every time ordering chicken vindaloo with basmati rice, Stoney, once he got used to the place, making a nuisance of himself, saying to Najim, the waiter, 'What about one of those dishes that sizzles when you bring it to the table?' Najim saying, 'How they do that, sir, they sprinkle a little cold water on the hot oil. If you wish, I can bring you a dry dish, chicken or lamb tandoori, perhaps, and sprinkle water on it?' Smiling at Grace as he spoke. Stoney not sure if Najim was taking the piss. Another time, just before Grace kicked him out, Stoney had asked if they had anything balti. Najim wasn't on that night. The waiter who served them saying there had been a terrible family tragedy. Najim's sister, his little niece and nephew all dead in a house fire. Their husband, Najim's brother-in-law, still too ill in hospital to be told that his family had perished.

Stoney deciding, This is not the right time.

Passing on the balti.

Grace finding it difficult to imagine.

Losing your whole family?

Saying to herself, Still, what you don't have, you can't miss.

Saying, now, to Sara.

As in tiara.

'I want to book a holiday abroad.'

Then: 'Somewhere sunny.'

Sara Cusson saying, 'Did you have any specific destination in mind?'

'I though maybe Hawaii.'

Sara Cusson saying, 'Hawaii?'

Not hiding her surprise.

Then, turning to her computer terminal, taking Grace's particulars. Full name, Grace always embarrassed, having to tell people her middle name, Ava, after the film star, Ava Gardner, her address in Popes Avenue. Grace saying, 'But, I won't still be living there by the time I go away.'

'I'm not with you?'

'I'll have sold the house by then.'

Remembering the estate agent's representative saying, after Grace had told him she was not interested in looking at other properties…

Up-scale.

Down-scale.

Grace thinking, at first, he was talking about kettles…

'I see, releasing funds… realising some of your capital.'

Grace, still free of the whisky, realising a lot of things.

Saying to Sara Cusson: 'There was a programme on the box last Tuesday, about Tiger Sharks… that was set in Hawaii. And you're too young to remember *From Here to Eternity*, Burt Lancaster and Deborah Kerr kissing on the beach, just before the war started. I've wanted to go to Hawaii one day… ever since I saw that picture.'

Remembering what Stoney always called Burt Lancaster.

Burt Lung Cancer.

Sara Cusson saying, 'Catch me in the water where there are sharks.'

Grace saying, 'I don't swim.'

Sara Cusson, busy with her computer, then saying, 'We can do a three week Winter Break. Nineteen hundred pounds, including flights, transfers, half-board accommodation at a three star hotel. As an optional extra, you might want to stop over in LA. Two nights, that would be an additional two hundred and eighty pounds.'

Then: 'How many of you will be travelling?'

Grace saying, 'I only want one way.'

'I'm sorry?'

'I want a single.'

Sara Cusson sighing, saying, 'I'm afraid, if you want it open-ended, we can arrange is a scheduled flight out… hotel bookings etcetera, will all be additional. It will work out much more expensive.'

Then: 'There also may be a problem with your visa application. The US immigration authorities will need to know that you have a home, a job, a family to return to here in England.'

Grace thinking, Home, job, family?

Why should she go away, anyway, she had all those things?

Saying, 'Visa?'

'For your passport… you will need a visa.'

Grace saying, 'Passport?'

Sara.

As in tiara.

Saying, 'You do have a passport?'

39

Darren feeling sick as a dog – or, was it parrot? – stomach churning, making all kinds of fucking racket, his mind jumping from one possibility to another, shit-scared, hoping Dennis wouldn't notice, thinking:

Is this for real?

Is my life for real?

Round his old lady's earlier, out in Hanwell. Semi-detached, bay windows, nice sized garden front and back, garage at the side, all his mother ever used to dream of while the old man was still alive creating havoc with their lives. Darren's stepfather, Tim, opening the door, pipe, cardigan, his mother a pace behind, saying, 'Who is it, dear?' Looking over Tim's shoulder, through the pipe smoke, seeing it was Darren, saying, 'There have been all kinds of people round looking for you.'

Darren thinking he would have preferred the usual 'Hello stranger', saying, 'What kind of people?'

His mother saying, 'Are you in some kind of trouble?'

Darren saying, 'Don't be daft, mother.'

Then: 'Are you going to let me in, or what?'

Already, knowing he couldn't ask.

Knowing he couldn't stay.

Not even one night.

Now, in the Mason's Arms, off-loading Frank Gill on to Dennis.

Fifteen hundred of the five thousand Terry Reece-Morgan had offered him, Terry Reece-Morgan saying, 'I don't have to be doing this, you know… you owe me, big time.'

Dennis with the gun.

Whole of fucking Acton probably knew by now.

Kevin at the bar, through complaining about his dead marine fish, what he intended doing to Monica only she was pregnant, totally out of it, explaining to Ted how to make a depth-charge.

Stoney, just come from Grace's, seen the FOR SALE sign.

Face like a wet week.

Darren saying to Dennis, 'Well, are you up for it, or what?'

Kevin, saying to Ted, 'You pour the lager, pint glass, right… then you take a shot glass, fill it with vodka, drop it carefully into the glass of lager, trying not to spill any on the way down. Shot glass settles on the bottom, bingo, you got your depth-charge.

Ted saying, 'You're pulling my pecker.'

Kevin saying, 'Dream on, sunshine.'

Darren saying to Dennis, 'I still remember it, Dennis, how we all used to look up to you. Like a fucking God, you were.'

And: 'Where did it all go wrong? Was it that tart, when she left you? Elaine, wasn't it? Ran off with that-drug salesman? What a carry on that was.'

Dennis remembering saying, 'Pregnant? How?'

The most stupid two words he had ever spoken.

Saying, now, to Darren, 'You were always talk, talk, talk, Darren. That's always been your trouble.'

Darren remembering the last time.

How he was going to do Dennis.

Give him what for.

Darren saying to Stoney, 'And as for you, you daft git. What is it with you and that old lady? You gone soft, or something?'

Stoney saying, 'You're a nutter, Darren.'

Then: 'A fucking nutter.'

Kevin coming across to their table with his depth-charge, saying, 'Witness this, lads.'

Dennis saying to Darren, 'I can't help but agree with Stoney, here, Darren. Fucking nutter just about sums it up.'

The last time.

Kiren on the mobile.

Whispering 'Angel-face.'

This time, Darren picking up the glass ash-tray, cigarette

butts spilling across the table, swinging it into the side of Dennis's face, connecting just above his eye, blood everywhere, chairs going over...

Darren feeling better than he had felt for days.

40.

Kiren laying around the flat, early evening, wanting to feel slinky, just taken an hour and a half deciding between the silk crepe georgette dress by Givenchy from Harvey Nick's and the Dolce and Gabbana black wrap mini-dress. Finally, going for the Givenchy, loving the idea of a dress, set her father back close to four thousand, still you felt naked.

Every so often taking a look in the mirror.
Studying the black eye.
Rolling a J.
Glass of white wine.
Thinking, Geurlain's *Midnight Secret* might be okay after a night on the tiles and a hang-over but it was precious bloody use when your boyfriend – ex-boyfriend – has smacked you one in the face.

Listening, now, to Darren's voice on the answerphone.
Four messages.
Hearing the first one, Kiren wishing that Darren was here in the room with her... so she could kick him in the teeth: 'Hey! Babe! This is you Angel Face, remember me? I'm the one who cares, the one who knows how to do it to you just the way you like it. Call me on the mobile number, why don't you?'

Hey?
Babe?
Darren had never called her babe before.
Not once.
Ever.
Maybe, he was cracking up.

The second message, Darren remembered to say that he was sorry.

The third, Kiren wanted to throw up, right there and then, Darren saying, 'Just say it to yourself... just admit you miss me just an itsy-witsy teensy-weensy bit.'

Jesus Christ!

The last was twenty-four hours later, no messing, straight to the point: 'Fuck you, bitch!'

Kiren deciding she preferred angry to pathetic.

Ringing his number to say, 'Fuck you, too,' but a recorded voice telling her Darren's number was unavailable.

Temporarily.

Turning on the Sony Trinitron.

Two fat cooks.

Kiren feeling sick, again, just looking at them, let alone what it was they were cooking... spilling white wine on the Givenchy dress, then hot ash from her third J spilling onto her thigh, burning into the crepe fabric. Kiren thinking, Sorry, daddy. Deciding she was through living off his money... give some body else a turn. Remembering what the divine Tara had said on the subject of boyfriends: 'Put it this way, when I board an aircraft I don't expect to be turning right.'

Then, feeling the wetness between her thighs. Kiren going to the bathroom, washing, finding the new box of tampons, changing out of the Givenchy, white crew-neck, Marks and Sparks, baggy, to her knees... enjoying the feel of soft wool against her flesh... La Perla's, red brocade sandals.

Nothing else.

In a hurry, now.

Anxious to make the call.

Body Form ad on the television.

Timing, right?

Remembering Darren saying, 'How can they sing shit like that with such feeling?'

And: 'It's offensive... an insult to every genuine soul singer ever walked this planet.'

And: 'A travesty.'

Kiren saying, 'Take it easy, Darren. It's only an advert.'

Ringing Reggie Crystal's number.

Reggie picking up on the third ring.
Kiren saying, 'I thought you'd like to know… I just came on.'
Reggie saying nothing.
Kiren saying, 'I split with Darren.'
Reggie saying, 'I heard.'
Then: 'Should I sympathise?'
'While you're swinging, I can hold the chair.'
'Can I trust you?'
'Can you trust anybody?'
Reggie saying, *'Then I said Hi! like a spider to the fly…'*
Kiren saying, 'What?'
'B-side. Old Rolling Stones single. I bet you're too young to remember The Rolling Stones?'
Kiren saying, 'B-side? What's a B-side?'

41

In the Mason's car park.
Darren staring at the empty space where the Jaguar had been parked, saying, 'Fucking stroll-on!'
And: 'Do I need this? Do I *really* need this?
'Fucking bastards!'
Patricia Weller.
Pronounced, Patric-*are* Well-*are*.
Norton-Hamblin Financing.
Finally tracked down the motor.
Darren saying, again, 'Fucking bastards!'
It wasn't asking much.
Saying to Terry Reece-Morgan, 'Up front?'
On the five thousand.
Terry Reece-Morgan saying, 'Don't push your luck, Darren.'
Now Dennis coming out the back door next to the fire escape, empty kegs piled up high in the shadows, Stoney and Kevin both with him.
Stoney saying, 'Let it rest, Dennis.'
Kevin saying, 'The fucker is not worth it.'
Dennis raising the gun.
Darren thinking, Oh shit!
About to put his hands up.
Seen too many films.
The explosion ripping into the night.
Dennis howling.
His right arm pumping blood.
Like water from a hose-pipe.

Kevin shouting, 'Grab a hold of him, for fuck's sake! He'll bleed to death!'

Stoney flapping his arms around.

Dennis running in circles.

Darren laughing.

Thinking, Well, sod your luck, Dennis.

Gun blowing up in your own fucking face.

42

Terry Reece-Morgan realising straight away what Reggie Crystal was doing at the reading of the will, the two of them sitting there… stiff-backed chairs, arms folded, both in suits, his solicitor, Alwyn Strong – surviving partner in Mayhew, Bosthwick and Strong, upstairs office suite in Turnham Green Terrace, opposite the wood yard – not even started on: 'I Rosemary Dorothy Jane Reece-Morgan, being of sound mind…'

Wondering why Rosy had bothered with a will.

Only forty-two.

Couldn't have expected to die.

The two of them, afterwards, Pizza Express in the High Road, Reggie with an American Hot, Terry Four Seasons, Reggie saying, 'Not for us to fathom the workings of the female mind.'

Signalling the waiter for more pepper.

Fresh ground.

Terry saying, 'You're a bastard, you do know that?'

Reggie raising his glass of red, saying, 'To us, Terry… to a long and successful association.'

Then: 'Like they say, Always run with the villains. That way, you know where you stand.'

'I was fucking blind.'

'You were in Spain, Terry… not taking care of business.'

'Frank Gill?'

'My pockets are deep.'

Then: 'You do have an option. You can always piss off back to Malaga… non-executive director, live off the dividend.'

'What would I do with myself?'

'I should leave that to the Spanish boys.'

Terry saying, 'Were you screwing Rosy?'

Reggie forking the Pepperoni sausage, four, five, six slices, putting them in his mouth, thinking about Kiren last night, Kiren saying, 'Any fantasy at all, Reggie, just name it.'

Reggie saying, 'Why are you frightened?'

Kiren saying, 'I want to be.'

Reggie musing that it wasn't often in this world he was able – or willing – to give a fellow human being exactly what it was they wanted.

Saying, 'You wearing a tampon?'

'I told you.'

'Givenchy? Versace? Prada?'

'There is no such thing as a designer tampon.'

'Not yet, there isn't.'

Saying, 'Your clean teamer days are over, Kiren. Starting now.'

Watching Terry Reece-Morgan playing with his pizza.

Thinking, Welsh fuck-wit.

Toss-pot.

Thinking, Class will out.

Picking sausage from his teeth.

Edge of his nail.

Little finger.

Saying, 'Screwing Rosemary? Do me a favour.'

43

At the funeral, the cremation, Mortlake Crematorium, the cortege retracing the route of Duncan's final car journey, Lindsay's colleagues from work, her mother and father down from Northampton, catching the four-thirty back, all of them remarking to each other how well Lindsay appeared to be bearing up. Lindsay realising that she was 'bearing up' only because she could not yet appreciate the profound calamity that had befallen her... that Duncan, *her* Duncan, was dead.

Foot of the stairs.

Lindsay home at two-thirty.

'Aneurysm.'

The doctors said.

The police finding the Fiat Panda at the corner of Sutton Court Road, piecing together events, the aneurysm a direct result of the car crash, Duncan thrown forward against the steering wheel, the police asking, 'Your husband usually not wear his seat-belt?'

Unable to explain.

How unlike Duncan that was...

The young black couple knocking – Lindsay thinking, *Definitely* a couple – asking after Duncan, saying they had bumped into him outside the night before, saw him to his front door, one of them saying, 'Was he out of it, or what.' The other saying, 'We're three doors down, how can you put *up* with that racket?' Then, when Lindsay told them, saying, 'Dead?'

Duncan's party piece.

Monty Python.

The Dead Parrot sketch.

Duncan knew it line for line, both parts, John Cleese *and* Michael Palin.

'This parrot has passed on, has ceased to be, expired and gone to meet its maker... this is a late parrot, a stiff, bereft of life, it rests in peace, has rung down the curtain and joined the choir invisible...

'...This is an ex-parrot.'

Only, it wasn't a parrot.

It was Duncan.

Saying to the two men, 'Well, thank you for your help, anyway.'

The two men concerned that they had not done more.

Lindsay saying, 'No, really.'

The police saying, 'Your husband? Like a drink, did he?'

Again, unable to explain.

Wanting to say that this was not Duncan.

Not Duncan at all.

Wanting to say, He was in love. Infatuated with a young girl... obsessed, making a complete and utter fool of himself. *That* was why he wasn't wearing his seat-belt. Why he was as drunk as a Lord. Why he was sitting at the foot of the stairs, his femoral artery distended like a flawed inner tube, then, moments before Lindsay arrived home, the artery bursting, flooding Duncan's body, Duncan drowning in his own blood.

The police saying, 'In the light of events, there will be no formal prosecution.'

Posthumous.

Lindsay saying, 'Well, I *am* grateful to hear that.'

Thinking, For foolishness over and beyond the call of middle-age...

The judge donning his square of black cloth.

The police saying, 'Mrs Ross? Are you all right?'

Lindsay saying, 'Should I be?'

The funeral service almost complete.

Sermon by numbers, the vicar inserting Duncan's name as and when necessary, piped organ music playing 'Abide With Me', Lindsay wondering if she should have briefed the vicar, offered some particular details from Duncan's life. The vicar saying, 'While we must mourn Duncan's passing, we must also remember to celebrate his life, pause a moment to consider how, in knowing him, he enriched our own lives.' Lindsay noticing three people she didn't recognise, assuming they were Duncan's colleagues from the newspaper, two men, both in their thirties, and a young girl. Realising the girl must be Carol.

Surprised at how ordinary she looked.

Not plain.

But, not beautiful, either.

The vicar saying, '... his short time here on earth...'

Lindsay thinking, Brief the vicar?

Particular details?

For instance, how Duncan once drew a chalk circle around a dog shit on the pavement outside their house, wrote next to it, with an arrow pointing at the shit: *What this dog-owner has for brains!*

Should she have told the vicar that?

Or, how he photographed rubbish in the street, intending to send prints to the council, but never did.

Or, how he would shout out of the window at motorists who drew up in the road, beeped their horns, a habit caught on through mini-cabs, Duncan shouting, 'Did you never hear of door bells?'

Paper on the toilet seat.

Despite, there was just the two of them.

Wiping his cutlery.

Holding his glass to the light.

Smelling the milk...

Every single time.

Duncan as an old fart.

Duncan.

Dead?

Womanising drunken driver?

A total distortion of his life realised in the manner of his death.

Wondering if the young girl, Carol, knew what an old fart Duncan had been.

Lindsay turning her head, looking back down the aisle as

the velvet curtains opened, the coffin began moving, seeing the girl, head buried in her hands, sobbing.

Lindsay wondering if they had.

And, if so, how often.

Wondering if Duncan had been a more enthusiastic lover with her than he had been with Lindsay, not knowing if that lack of enthusiasm was Duncan's fault or her own.

Realising that the girl held a secret.

The coffin gone.

Lindsay not wanting to know the answer.

Suddenly, aware that Jane was not at the service.

Not guilt, surely?

The doctor assuring Lindsay, 'There was nothing you could have possibly done.'

The night of Duncan's death, Jane and Lindsay sharing two bottles of South African chardonnay, Cardinal's Wine Bar, in Devonshire Road. An evening of enjoyable self-commiseration, the men in their lives, their work at the CSA... Jane saying how unfair it all was, that the work they took on board, how different was it from the work of a solicitor in matrimonial practice? How, in fact, their role at the agency had superseded the function of the divorce lawyer in arriving at equitable settlements.

And how much did they earn?

Compared to a solicitor.

Both of them tipsy.

Lindsay not sure how it had happened...

That first kiss.

Tongues.

Had it been her tongue first, or Jane's?

The sheer physical shock.

Electricity.

Jane saying, 'Did you ever? Before?'

Her hand on Lindsay's thigh beneath the table.

Lindsay saying, 'No offence, Jane, but I doubt I would enjoy this any more than I do with men.'

44

Reggie Crystal, Terry Reece-Morgan and Darren on the shingle beach at Whitstable, the beach sloping away steeply, Darren having trouble staying on his feet, stones sliding out from under him, saying, 'Well, that was all very nice of you chaps.'

Then: 'Long way to go for a plate of fish and chips, though.'

The three of them hearing the sea but not able to see it in the darkness. Terry Reece-Morgan, imagining the grey-flecked waves, pointing, his arm fully stretched, saying, 'Over there, those lights, that must be Canvey Island.'

Reggie saying, 'We'd be too far west. That's Southend. On a clear night, straight over would be Clacton.'

Across the water.

Mouth of the Thames Estuary.

On the way down Reggie, being Reggie, giving them all the local colour, saying: 'One of the Krays owns the pub across from where we'll be eating.'

And: 'Lots of East Enders moved out this way after the war... used to call it Whitstabubble.'

And: 'Peter Cushing lived in Whitstable. There's a bench on the sea wall donated by Peter Cushing and his wife, Helen. She'd been gone eleven years by then, but, he still liked to include her in on everything. There's a plaque, too, Cushing's View. After his wife died he used to like to just sit there staring out to sea.'

And: 'There's a pub, Alberres, they have a line drawn four feet up on the wall, marks how high the water rose in the big flood of '52.'

All this before they had got out of London, reached the M2.

Terry Reece-Morgan, from the back seat, saying, 'Old Kent Road? About time they built a fucking New Kent Road.'

Reggie saying, 'As it happens, Terry, they did.'

The stretch from the Elephant, through New Cross, to Shooters Hill all stopping and starting, taking for ever.

South-east London.

Terry saying, 'The tourists straight of the ferry have to work their way through this lot.'

Darren saying, 'Fucking good job... might put some of the bastards off coming.'

Reggie's Turbo R drawing glances from the pavement.

Reggie, joking, saying, ' Baton down the hatches, lads, we're about to get car-jacked.'

An hour later, coming through Saltdean, the shantytown bungalows along the front, Reggie spotting a notice in a pub window: *No hop-pickers.*

Made his day.

Reggie, on the beach, now, saying, 'Fish and chips? You are a fucking pleb, Darren.'

Then: 'Normally you would need to book months ahead for that place.'

The Oyster Bar and Clubhouse.

Right on the beach.

Outside, in the summer, blue and white striped canvas awnings, tables out along the sea wall... Inside, all unsanded floors, mis-matched tables, cooler cabinets of beer, white wine and mineral water, display counters piled high with iced oysters, langoustine, cock crab, lobsters, chalk boards spaced around the white walls showing the day's menu, starters and main courses, sweets on a separate board. Whitstable, stuck in time, not an amusement arcade between here and Margate, smart folks up from London, come down to eat fish, pretend they are across the Channel in Normandy.

Reggie saying, 'Fucking goldmine.'

Table booked for eight o'clock, they were out by ten-thirty. Reggie ordering the baked halibut with Gruyere cheese and mustard, Terry having the monkfish medallions with garlic and rosemary, Darren sticking with the plaice and chips – *Deep fried plaice in beer batter*, it said on the chalk board – Darren saying, 'If this is local caught, I'm a dead man, state of that fucking water outside.'

Reggie saying, 'You ordered it, Darren.'

Darren saying, 'A joke, Reggie... it was supposed to be a joke.'

Terry saying, 'Ha-bloody-ha.'

Wondering why they were bothering with this shit.

Saying to Reggie, earlier, 'Let's just fucking do it!'

Reggie saying to Darren, now, 'You do realise, don't you, Darren, just how much bother you have caused of late?'

Then: 'We will need to suspend a number of initiatives till this all blows over.'

'This all' being Darren's current problems.

Dennis in hospital, stump for a right hand, like some fucking Arab caught with his hand in the till.

The Webley service revolver.

Police making the connection.

The old man, whose gun it was, making a right song and dance...

Not to mention, Rosemary.

And Darren's problems with the bailiffs.

Reggie saying, 'Never rains but it pours, eh, Darren?'

Terry Reece-Morgan saying, 'A liability, Darren. No two ways about it.'

Then: 'You should see this place in the daylight... swim here, you'd need your stomach pumped for a week.'

Darren saying, 'Didn't I just say that? About the fish?'

Thinking, The King never ate fish... just burgers and deep fried sandwiches, peanut butter and banana. Never deserted his roots, no matter how much money he made. Too much of a good ol' boy to get into all that fancy cooking.

Cracker to the end.

Darren seeing Elvis there on the bathroom floor, crouched like a frog, head turned sideways, resting on his hands, face blue, tongue lolling out of his mouth... how his fiancée, Ginger Alden, found him.

When he died.

Two hundred and fifty pounds.

Darren working it out, once.
Near enough eighteen stone.

A local approaching along the shingle, hearing him before they saw him, zip-up car coat, hat and scarf, walking the dog, a black miniature poodle, you could hardly see it in the dark.

The man saying, 'Evening.'
Then: 'They say there'll be more rain, later.'
Darren saying, 'Oh, do they?'
Thinking, Boring fuck.
Then, thinking of Kiren.
That way she had of rotating her hips.
Couldn't help but come, when she did that.
Staring into his face.
Lazy smile.
Since my baby left me I've found a new place to dwell,
It's at the end of Lonely Street, called...
Thinking, What the fuck am I doing in Whitstable?

The miniature poodle sniffing at Terry Reece-Morgan's trouser leg. Darren turning towards the sea, staring out into the darkness, feeling like a fuck-wit, suddenly coming up with an idea that crazy.

Reggie?
Terry?
No way.
Not quite hearing the report.
Like when you wake yourself snoring.
Thinking, In swim not mine...
A nanosecond
Between sentience
And extinction.

45

The Cortina 2.00 GL, X Reg sitting outside in the road, Banham Street, coachwork gleaming, as good as new, Mrs M saying to Stoney, 'All right, I suppose, if you like old bangers.'

Kevin dropped it off from the garage this morning.
Been working on it all week.
Electrics.
Rebore.
Spot-welding on the sub-frame.
Body, sills.
New tyres.
Respray, the original Olive Green.
MOT.
Taxed.
Fully comprehensive insurance.
Stoney saying, 'Well, fuck me.'
Mrs M saying, 'Language!'
Kevin saying, 'Courtesy of Grace.'
Stoney saying, 'She sold the house, then?'
Kevin saying, 'I did her a price, it being Grace.'
Then: 'Stoney… get a grip, will you? Not out here.'
Stoney saying, 'I can't help it.'
Mrs M saying, 'Big baby you are… Let's go in. I'll get the kettle on.'

BLOODLINES the cutting-edge crime and mystery imprint…

Perhaps She'll Die! by John B Spencer
Giles could never say 'no' to a woman… any woman. But when he tangled with Celeste, he made a mistake… A bad mistake.
Celeste was married to Harry, and Harry walked a dark side of the street that Giles – with his comfortable lifestyle and fashionable media job – could only imagine in his worst nightmares. And when Harry got involved in nightmares, people had a habit of getting hurt.
Set against the boom and gloom of Eighties Britain, *Perhaps She'll Die!* is classic *noir* with a centre as hard as toughened diamond.
ISBN 1 899344 14 4 – £5.99

Quake City by John B Spencer
The third novel to feature Charley Case, the hard-boiled investigator of a future that follows the 'Big One of Ninety-Seven' – the quake that literally rips California apart and makes LA an Island.
'Classic Chandleresque private eye tale, jazzed up by being set in the future… but some things never change – PI Charley Case still has trouble with women and a trusty bottle of bourbon is always at hand. An entertaining addition to the private eye canon.' – *Mail on Sunday*
ISBN 1 899344 02 0 – £5.99

Smalltime by Jerry Raine
Smalltime is a taut, psychological crime thriller, set among the seedy world of petty criminals and no-hopers. In this remarkable début, Jerry Raine shows just how easily curiosity can turn into fear amid the horrors, despair and despondency of life lived a little too near the edge.
'Jerry Raine's *Smalltime* carries the authentic whiff of sleazy Nineties Britain. He vividly captures the world of stunted ambitions and their evil consequences.' – Simon Brett
'The first British contemporary crime novel featuring an underclass which no one wants. Absolutely authentic and quite possibly important.' – Philip Oakes, *Literary Review*. ISBN 1 899344 13 6 – £5.99

BLOODLINES the cutting-edge crime and mystery imprint...

The Hackman Blues by Ken Bruen

'If Martin Amis was writing crime novels, this is what he would hope to write.' – *Books in Ireland*

'...I haven't taken my medication for the past week. If I couldn't go a few days without the lithium, I was in deep shit. I'd gotten the job ten days earlier and it entailed a whack of pub-crawling. Booze and medication is the worst of songs. Sing that!

A job of pure simplicity. Find a white girl in Brixton. Piece of cake. What I should have done is doubled my medication and lit a candle to St Jude – maybe a lot of candles.'

Add to the mixture a lethal ex-con, an Irish builder obsessed with Gene Hackman, the biggest funeral Brixton has ever seen, and what you get is the Blues like they've never been sung before.

Ken Bruen's powerful second novel is a gritty and grainy mix of crime noir and Urban Blues that greets you like a mugger stays with you like a razor-scar.

GQ described his début novel as:

'The most startling and original crime novel of the decade.'

The Hackman Blues is Ken Bruen's best novel yet.

Fresh Blood II edited by Mike Ripley & Maxim Jakubowski

Follow-up to the highly-acclaimed original volume (see below), featuring short stories from John Baker, Christopher Brookmyre, Ken Bruen, Carol Anne Davis, Christine Green, Lauren Henderson, Charles Higson, Maxim Jakubowski, Phil Lovesey, Mike Ripley, Iain Sinclair, John Tilsley, John Williams, and RD Wingfield (Inspector Frost).

Fresh Blood edited by Mike Ripley & Maxim Jakubowski

Featuring the cream of the British New Wave of crime writers including John Harvey, Mark Timlin, Chaz Brenchley, Russell James, Stella Duffy, Ian Rankin, Nicholas Blincoe, Joe Canzius, Denise Danks, John B Spencer, Graeme Gordon, and a previously unpublished extract from the late Derek Raymond. Includes an introduction from each author explaining their views on crime fiction in the '90s and a comprehensive foreword on the genre from Angel-creator, Mike Ripley. ISBN 1 899344 03 9 – £6.99

BLOODLINES the cutting-edge crime and mystery imprint...

That Angel Look by Mike Ripley

'The outrageous, rip-roarious Mr Ripley is an abiding delight...'
– Colin Dexter

A chance encounter (in a pub, of course) lands street-wise, cab-driving Angel the ideal job as an all-purpose assistant to a trio of young and very sexy fashion designers.

But things are nowhere near as straightforward as they should be and it soon becomes apparent that no-one is telling the truth – least of all Angel! Double-cross turns to triple-cross and Angel finds himself set-up by friend and enemy alike. This time, Angel could really meet his match...

'I never read Ripley on trains, planes or buses. He makes me laugh and it annoys the other passengers.' – Minette Walters.

1 899344 23 3 – £8

I Love The Sound of Breaking Glass by Paul Charles

First outing for Irish-born Detective Inspector Christy Kennedy whose beat is Camden Town, north London. Peter O'Browne, managing director of Camden Town Records, is missing. Is his disappearance connected with a mysterious fire that ravages his north London home? And just who was using his credit card in darkest Dorset?

Although up to his neck in other cases, Detective Inspector Christy Kennedy and his team investigate, plumbing the hidden depths of London's music industry, turning up murder, chart-rigging scams, blackmail and worse. *I Love The Sound of Breaking Glass* is a detective story with a difference. Part whodunnit, part howdunnit and part love story, it features a unique method of murder, a plot with more twists and turns than the road from Kingsmarkham to St Mary Mead.

Paul Charles is one of Europe's best known music promoters and agents. In this, his stunning début, he reveals himself as master of the crime novel. ISBN 1 899344 16 0 – £7

Shrouded by Carol Anne Davis

Douglas likes women — quiet women; the kind he deals with at the mortuary where he works. Douglas meets Marjorie, unemployed, gaining weight and losing confidence. She talks and laughs a lot to cover up her shyness, but what Douglas really needs is a lover who'll stay still — deadly still. Driven by lust and fear, Douglas finds a way to make girls remain excitingly silent and inert. But then he is forced to blank out the details of their unplanned deaths.

Perhaps only Marjorie can fulfil his growing sexual hunger. If he could just get her into a state of limbo. Douglas studies his textbooks to find a way...

Shrouded is a powerful and accomplished début, tautly-plotted, dangerously erotic and vibrating with tension and suspense.

ISBN 1 899344 17 9 — £7

Outstanding Paperback Fiction from The Do-Not Press:

Elvis – The Novel by Robert Graham, Keith Baty
'Quite simply, the greatest music book ever written'
— Mick Mercer, *Melody Maker*
The everyday tale of an imaginary superstar eccentric. The Presley neither his fans nor anyone else knew. First-born of triplets, he came from the backwoods of Tennessee. Driven by a burning ambition to sing opera, Fate sidetracked him into creating Rock 'n' roll.
His classic movie, *Driving A Sportscar Down To A Beach In Hawaii* didn't win the Oscar he yearned for, but The Beatles revived his flagging spirits, and he stunned the world with a guest appearance in Batman.
Further shockingly momentous events have led him to the peaceful, contented lifestyle he enjoys today.
'Books like this are few and far between.' – Charles Shaar Murray, *NME*
ISBN 1 899344 19 5 – £7

The Users by Brian Case
The welcome return of Brian Case's brilliantly original '60s cult classic.
'A remarkable debut' – Anthony Burgess
'Why Case's spiky first novel from 1968 should have languished for nearly thirty years without a reprint must be one of the enigmas of modern publishing. Mercilessly funny and swaggeringly self-conscious, it could almost be a template for an early Martin Amis.' – *Sunday Times*.
ISBN 1 899344 05 5 – £5.99

Charlie's Choice: The First Charlie Muffin Omnibus by Brian Freemantle – *Charlie Muffin; Clap Hands, Here Comes Charlie; The Inscrutable Charlie Muffin*
Charlie Muffin is not everybody's idea of the ideal espionage agent. Dishevelled, cantankerous and disrespectful, he refuses to play by the Establishment's rules. Charlie's axiom is to screw anyone from anywhere to avoid it happening to him. But it's not long before he finds himself offered up as an unwilling sacrifice by a disgraced Department, desperate to win points in a ruthless Cold War. Now for the first time, the first three Charlie Muffin books are collected together in one volume.
'Charlie is a marvellous creation' – *Daily Mail*

Also available in paperback from The Do-Not Press

Dancing With Mermaids
by Miles Gibson

'Absolutely first rate. Absolutely wonderful' – Ray Bradbury
Strange things are afoot in the Dorset fishing town of Rams Horn.
Set close to the poisonous swamps at the mouth of the River Sheep, the town has been isolated from its neighbours for centuries.
But mysterious events are unfolding… A seer who has waited for years for her drowned husband to reappear is haunted by demons, an African sailor arrives from the sea and takes refuge with a widow and her idiot daughter. Young boys plot sexual crimes and the doctor, unhinged by his desire for a woman he cannot have, turns to a medicine older than his own.

'An imaginative tour de force and a considerable stylistic achievement. When it comes to pulling one into a world of his own making, Gibson has few equals among his contemporaries.'
– *Time Out*

'A wild, poetic exhalation that sparkles and hoots and flies.'
– *The New Yorker*

'An extraordinary talent dances with perfect control across hypnotic page.' – *Financial Times*

ISBN 1 899344 25 X – £7

The Sandman
by Miles Gibson

"*I am the Sandman. I am the butcher in soft rubber gloves. I am the acrobat called death.*
I am the fear in the dark. I am the gift of sleep…"
Growing up in a small hotel in a shabby seaside town, Mackerel Burton has no idea that he is to grow up to become a slick and ruthless serial killer. A lonely boy, he amuses himself by perfecting his conjuring tricks, but slowly the magic turns to a darker kind, and soon he finds himself stalking the streets of London in search of random and innocent victims. He has become The Sandman.

'A truly remarkable insight into the workings of a deranged mind: a vivid, extraordinarily powerful novel which will grip you to the end and which you'll long remember' – *Mystery & Thriller Guild*

'A horribly deft piece of work!" – *Cosmopolitan*

'Written by a virtuoso – it luxuriates in death with a Jacobean fervour'
– *The Sydney Morning Herald*

'Confounds received notions of good taste – unspeakable acts are reported with an unwavering reasonableness essential to the comic impact and attesting to the deftness of Gibson's control.'
– *Times Literary Supplement*

ISBN 1 899344 24 1 – £7

Outstanding Paperback Originals from The Do-Not Press:

It's Not A Runner Bean by Mark Steel

'I've never liked Mark Steel and I thoroughly resent the high quality of this book.' – Jack Dee

The life of a Slightly Successful Comedian can include a night spent on bare floorboards next to a pyromaniac squatter in Newcastle, followed by a day in Chichester with someone so aristocratic, they speak without ever moving their lips.

From his standpoint behind the microphone, Mark Steel is in the perfect position to view all human existence. Which is why this book – like his act, broadcasts and series' – is opinionated, passionate, and extremely funny. It even gets around to explaining the line (screamed at him by an Eighties yuppy): 'It's not a runner bean…' – which is another story.

'Hugely funny…' – *Time Out*

'A terrific book. I have never read any other book about comedy written by someone with a sense of humour.' – Jeremy Hardy, *Socialist Review*.
ISBN 1 899344 12 8– £5.99

It's You That I Want To Kiss by Maxim Jakubowski

They met among the torrid nightlife of Miami Beach, but soon they were running. From the Florida heat to rain-drenched Seattle, Anne and Jake blaze an unforgettable trail of fast sex, forbidden desires and sudden violence, pursued across America by a chilling psychopath.

Set against a backdrop of gaudy neon-lit American roadhouses and lonely highways, It's you that I want to kiss is a no-holds-barred rock 'n' roll road movie in print, in which every turn offers hidden danger, and where every stranger is a potential enemy. ISBN 1 899344 15 2 – £7.99

Life In The World Of Women

a collection of vile, dangerous and loving stories by Maxim Jakubowski

Maxim Jakubowski's dangerous and erotic stories of war between the sexes are collected here for the first time.

'Demonstrates that erotic fiction can be amusing, touching, spooky and even (at least occasionally) elegant. Erotic fiction seems to be Jakubowski's true metier. These stories have the hard sexy edge of Henry Miller and the redeeming grief of Jack Kerouac. A first class collection.'
– Ed Gorman, *Mystery Scene* (USA)
ISBN 1 899344 06 3 – £6.99

The Do-Not Press
Fiercely Independent Publishing

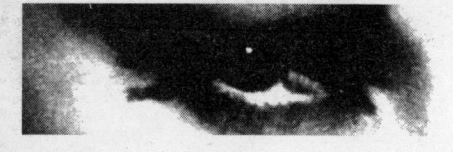

Keep in touch with what's happening at the cutting edge of independent British publishing.

Join The Do-Not Press Information Service and receive advance information of all our new titles, as well as news of events and launches in your area, and the occasional free gift and special offer. Simply send your name and address to:

The Do-Not Press (Dept. TAN)

PO Box 4215

London

SE23 2QD

or email us: thedonotpress@zoo.co.uk

There is no obligation to purchase and no salesman will call.

Visit our regularly-updated Internet site:

http://www.thedonotpress.co.uk

Mail Order

All our titles are available from good bookshops, or (in case of difficulty) direct from The Do-Not Press at the address above. There is no charge for post and packing. (NB: A postman may call.)